Other books by Deborah Blumenthal

Fat Chance

What Men Want

FAT CAMP

Deborah Blumenthal

nal
jam
books

NAL Jam
Published by New American Library, a division of
Penguin Group (USA) Inc., 375 Hudson Street,
New York, New York 10014, USA
Penguin Group (Canada), 90 Eglinton Avenue East, Suite 700, Toronto,
Ontario M4P 2Y3, Canada (a division of Pearson Penguin Canada Inc.)
Penguin Books Ltd., 80 Strand, London WC2R 0RL, England
Penguin Ireland, 25 St. Stephen's Green, Dublin 2,
Ireland (a division of Penguin Books Ltd.)
Penguin Group (Australia), 250 Camberwell Road, Camberwell, Victoria 3124,
Australia (a division of Pearson Australia Group Pty. Ltd.)
Penguin Books India Pvt. Ltd., 11 Community Centre, Panchsheel Park,
New Delhi - 110 017, India
Penguin Group (NZ), cnr Airborne and Rosedale Roads, Albany,
Auckland 1310, New Zealand (a division of Pearson New Zealand Ltd.)
Penguin Books (South Africa) (Pty.) Ltd., 24 Sturdee Avenue,
Rosebank, Johannesburg 2196, South Africa

Penguin Books Ltd., Registered Offices:
80 Strand, London WC2R 0RL, England

First published by NAL Jam, an imprint of New American Library,
a division of Penguin Group (USA) Inc.

First Printing, June 2006
10 9 8 7 6 5 4 3 2 1

NAL JAM and logo are trademarks of Penguin Group (USA) Inc.

LIBRARY OF CONGRESS CATALOGING-IN-PUBLICATION DATA:

Blumenthal, Deborah
Fat camp / Deborah Blumenthal.
p. cm.
Summary: At a summer camp for overweight teenagers, high school student Cam Phillips
finds support from her cabin mates and love from a fellow camper as she battles her weight
and her perceptions of food and exercise.
ISBN 0-451-21865-5
[1. Weight control—Fiction. 2. Camps—Fiction. 3. Friendship—Fiction.] I. Title.
PZ7.B6267Fat 2006
[Fic]—dc22   2005034336

Set in Berkeley Book
Designed by Ginger Legato

Printed in the United States of America

To Ralph

ACKNOWLEDGMENTS

With special thanks to my agent, Claudia Cross, and my editor, Anne Bohner, for their unswerving support and enthusiasm for this book.

ONE

The second reason that I'm happy to be sitting in an Upper East Side Manhattan diner is that the waiter with the buff build who's smiling down at me looks a lot like Chad Michael Murray, the TV hottie. The first reason is the bacon avocado Swiss cheeseburger, medium rare, sweet potato fries please, salad with blue cheese dressing, and a cherry Coke that *he's* going to bring me.

"Cam," my mom says in a world-weary tone, as she's tallying up the calories and triple-digit grams of fat in her head.

I look up in time to see my dad shoot her a *give her a break* look that I'm not supposed to see.

CMM nods and starts scribbling everything down in a little pad that fits into the palm of his hand. *And a date with you,* I'm tempted to add to see if he's really paying attention.

My farewell-to-food feast is taking place at EJ's Luncheonette, which is down the street from our apartment and next door to a boutique where wife beaters cost almost as much as an iPod and a drugstore that's open 24/7 for emergency chip-and-dip runs.

EJ's is a reincarnation of the diners that were popular before I was born, says my mom, a nostalgia buff. She gets almost misty-eyed when she describes the chrome trim on everything but the food, the way the counter stools were covered in vinyl with glittery silver slivers underneath, and how each table had its own little accordion-size jukebox where you could play three songs for a quarter.

None of that matters to me except that if they made hamburgers the way EJ's does—big, flat, and juicy, not round like meatballs—then I wouldn't have minded living then. I also like EJ's because the waiters are all cute and keep smiling even when bratty kids throw tantrums and drop open grilled-cheese sandwiches that fall face-down and stick to the floor.

Most of the waiters look like guys who are studying to

be actors but in the meantime have to pay their rent so take any night jobs they can get to keep from panhandling while they spend their days auditioning.

After taking my order, CMM turns to my mom, who tries unsuccessfully to look upbeat. She looks to my dad for support, but I think that he's more interested in staring at the twenty-something mom in the next booth who's wearing a tank top that does a pathetic job of covering her shaky boobs.

"Broiled salmon," she says to him, almost self-righteously. "With a baked potato and steamed spinach." My dad nods resignedly, as though her choice is fine with him too, although I'm sure that he'd rather pig out and say, "Way to go, make that two" after I order. CMM has already turned away when my mom calls after him.

"And no bread basket," she adds. He raises his thumb to let her know that he's heard.

So the family dinner with my mom, a best-selling novelist, and my dad, a criminal lawyer, is a farewell to New York City feast that will be followed by my last sleepover with my best friend, Evie, for an entire eight weeks—summer vacation—when I'm supposed to have *fun.*

Why?

Because tomorrow, I'll be leaving town.

"Camp . . . just a camp in the Berkshires," I told the

lunch table at school on the last day when we were talking about where we'd be spending the summer. "What else is there to say?"

Evie knows the truth, but I know that my secret's safe with her because aside from the fact that I'm overweight and she isn't, I think that the two of us are really halves of the same person and that somehow we got split apart at birth.

The camp where I'll be spending the summer, you see, isn't like the camps that everyone else I know will be going to. It's a special camp where every sport and every activity has an ulterior motive behind it: weight loss. There, I've said it.

I agreed to go only after my parents swore that if I spent eight weeks there and "tried" to lose weight and learn "how to eat well," they'd buy me a new laptop and *finally* get me a dog.

But I'm making it all simpler than it is.

To backtrack: Ever since I was born, I have had more fat cells than I should have. Nobody in the family can quite figure out why, since both my parents are slim—and work out every day of the week with a hunky, bulked-up personal trainer so that they'll stay that way. But somehow, through some freak of nature or something, I didn't inherit their thin genes, the kind that are made for sprouting bodies that fit into designer clothes. Bottom line, I was pudgy at birth and have been ever since.

Being pudgy, or whatever you want to call it (and don't ask me what I weigh, I'm *not* telling), didn't bother me much when I was growing up. I mean, when you're five, six, or seven you don't think about how you look or compare yourself to other kids. Mirrors are things that decorate the walls. You don't spend time studying yourself. You don't go to department stores and try on whisper-light thongs and then look in the three-way mirrors to see how fat your ass looks from the back and find out that it looks like the back of a bus.

But then you're thirteen, fourteen, or fifteen and everything changes. Your friends buy bikinis, but you can't—they don't fit—and if they do, you hate the repulsive way you look anyway (and let's face it, there are not many extra-extra-larges on the bikini rack). Other girls hook up with guys or at least get asked to the movies or to hang out, but you don't. You're "fat" and unpopular and have thunder thighs. When you hear guys whistle, you never turn around—it's not for you; in fact, you pray that they don't yell out something that would make you die of embarrassment.

So how do you deal? Sometimes you just sleep to feel

better, or hide in the bathroom and cry with the water running so that nobody hears. Other times you eat because it tastes good and makes you feel better and calmer, and screw it, why not just finish the quart of vanilla mint chip that goes down so easy, because it's all pretty hopeless anyway—you are the way you are—and at least pleasure comes in a carton.

So that's what I did, and that's what I do, and I don't know whether it's ever going to change. I don't look like a *Teen Vogue* model and never will, even though in my fantasies, I sometimes imagine that *maybe,* if I set my mind to it and honestly tried, I could, and then everything in my life would be different and I'd finally be happy.

But right now my mom insists that this "self-destructive cycle has to come to an end" or I'll be an "overweight and unhappy adult," so we had like an intervention with all of us and my shrink, and guess who came out on top?

Of course they didn't just decide out of the blue to try a weight-loss camp. First, I tried a gazillion times or more to "just use self-control." My record is about a week. After that, I start to feel like a drug addict in withdrawal, fixated on my next meal.

Once, though, we were on vacation in Italy, and the

hotel clerk was a total hottie. Motivated by the vision of him behind the concierge desk every morning and night, I was totally psyched to get him to focus on me. So for two solid weeks, I tried desperately to lose weight—and trust me, when you're in Italy, that's an eternity. Naturally, on day fourteen, after walking the streets all day, dragging from churches with frescoes, Madonnas, and altarpieces to museums with frescoes, Madonnas, and altarpieces, my determination vanished when we finally sat down to dinner at an outdoor café, at which point I was about to pass out from hunger. No WAY I was not ordering fritto misto, followed by pasta Alfredo, a bottle of Orangina, and, for dessert, to-die-for gelato.

Next attempt, the Weight Watchers' diet (where everybody who came to the meetings looked like fifty), because someone I IM with swore to me that it worked for her. So I tried to learn how to pick the foods that added up to the points I was allowed. But after a few weeks, I lost interest in tallying up the totals and I hate math anyway, so when my parents went out to dinner, I opened the Sub-Zero and stood there eating whatever the hell I wanted because it seemed pointless to count points.

One of the group leaders kept bragging about all the "freedom" that we had on WW, but I didn't see it that way. Naturally, when it came time to get weighed in, guess who didn't lose weight? Atkins followed, South Beach, macrobiotic, and then, well, you get the picture. . . .

My dad raises his glass of wine and begins to prepare a toast. I make a face at him, because I really hate these build-up-Cam's-ego family dramas.

"Dad," I say, closing my eyes and opening my mouth as if what he's about to say will make me barf. Just then, CMM arrives at the table with my cherry Coke, and I smile brightly at him and then drop my eyes and study him below the belt. My dad puts his glass down for a moment and places his hand over mine.

"Cut me a little slack," he says. "Your old man is going to miss his daughter." I roll my eyes slightly. The truth is, I'll probably miss him too, but I'd never admit it, because I hate these sentimental kind of speeches that leave everyone shifting in their seats and not looking at anyone else in the face.

"Okay," I say. "Let's toast and get it over with." He raises his glass again.

"To the best daughter in the world—our love, support, and encouragement. We hope that you have a transforming summer!"

"A transforming summer? Does that mean that in eight weeks I'm supposed to go from fat to thin?" What I do know we can count on is that this so-called camp will transform his wallet from fat to thin, because for what they're spending, we could have gone to Disneyland for a month and stayed at a five-star hotel with free all-you-can-eat buffet breakfasts.

"Becoming the best that you can be," he says, trying to explain. "But most of all, having fun and new experiences, and making good friends." My mom raises her glass of heart-healthy red wine and touches it to my Coke as CMM returns with a cheeseburger the size of a saucer. He places it in front of me while they get their fish. He pivots and comes back with a mountain of—mmmmm—spinach!

"Everything okay?" he asks, all innocence, after he places a red plastic basket filled with golden-brown sweet potato fries next to my cheeseburger.

I stare up into his perfect green eyes and don't say anything, hoping that at some level he'll understand.

"Fine," my mom says, and he turns, out of my life. My attention goes back to the aroma of freshly grilled beef and I reach for the ketchup. I shake it hard and pound the bottom so BOOM, a thick red river oozes out. I put the top of the toasted sesame bun back on and pat it, then wait just a moment before I lift it up to my watering mouth.

As I stare down at the plate, I'm suddenly overcome

with sadness. Why can't I be like everybody else? Why did I have to get the short end of the stick? For the next eight weeks, I'm going to be imprisoned in a place where spartan portions of fish, chicken, and pasta and free-for-alls of salad and veggies will take the place of real meals, happy meals. After this burger and fries, life as I have known it will be coming to an end. While everyone else I know will be carbing it up, feasting on mac and cheese, lasagna, and lumberjack breakfasts, not to mention make-your-own ice cream sundaes, yours truly will be in the gulag of self-denial.

Is that anything to drink to?

TWO

Every camp bus in the universe stops in front of the Metropolitan Museum of Art in Manhattan, and every parent in the universe has a picture of his kid, squinting in the sunlight, on the steps of the huge, boring museum (I mean the Temple of Dendur?) taken in the tense minutes before they tell you to get on the bus.

Some of the parents look euphoric about the idea of their kids going off to camp for a solid eight weeks, because as soon as they're gone, they're going to party. Then there are the parents wearing sunglasses with balled-up tissues in their fists who just look quiet and reflective, because for them being without their kids isn't going to be that much fun, or at least that's the idea that

they want their kids to hold onto. My parents? Somewhere in between.

I don't look at the other kids very hard, but don't think
I don't notice that most of them, like me, need to lose
weight, somewhere in the range of from twenty to fifty
pounds. As for me, twenty-five would be fine, but thirty-
five would be better. Of course, all of us know it. Nobody
here has on those really tight little Juicy T-shirts that are
supposed to showcase your tight abs. And nobody is
wearing clingy terry-cloth drawstring pants that hang low
on your hips so when you bend down the top of your
crack shows. What they're wearing are jeans or baggy
shorts and oversized T-shirts, and they're carrying back-
packs or shoulder bags that are so huge they can sub for
the trunks that were picked up about a year before they
needed to be.

"Cam Phillips?" A smiling counselor with long blond
hair and a clipboard pressed to her chest calls my name.
I raise my hand slightly.

"Great!" she says too enthusiastically for my taste.
What is so great about the fact that I've shown up for
the bus?

"Hello," my mom says to her, feeling for some reason
that she has to intervene. She offers her hand.

"I'm Cary Phillips, Cam's mom. It's so nice to meet you."

"Are you the . . ." Charlene says, pausing in awe as though she's being introduced to royalty. "The . . . writer?"

"Yes," my mom says softly, with a small smile.

"I just LOVED *Strange Alliances*. It was so incredible," she says, pronouncing it, "incred-a-bull."

Strange Alliances was my mom's last book—about a dysfunctional family. I don't think that she wrote it with the First Family in mind, but since she interviewed them for a *Vanity Fair* cover story, it went on to become a best-seller because everyone thought that's exactly what it was.

"Thank you," my mom says, velvety-voiced, then ducking out of the limelight, she asks, "Will you be one of Cam's counselors?"

"I'm in charge of the senior girls' counselors," she says. "So I'm really there for all the girls."

I'm sure that my mom notices that Charlene (printed in pink on her press-on name tag—those things alone are enough to make me despise the camp) most definitely does not have a weight problem. She's stick-thin, actually.

"How many counselors are there for each group?" my mom asks as if she's on some kind of fact-finding mission. What's she going to ask next, the square footage of the bunks? The location of the pine forest where they cut down the trees to build it?

"One for every five girls," Charlene says, "and then a

supervisor who watches over four groups." At that point I'm wondering whether I'm going to a camp or a maximum-security prison. Do they have watchtowers with armed guards so that no one will steal away and go into town for a feed?

"What if we don't like the group we're in?" I ask. "Can we change?"

"Cam, you're not even there yet," my mom says, "and you're thinking about switching out of your group?"

Yes, but I don't say that because I don't want Charlene to think that I'm Miss Doom and Gloom.

I shrug. "Just in case."

Just then my dad joins us. He has come from an emergency run to a coffee shop on Lexington Avenue where he had to buy bottled water because they were both worried about me dying of thirst on the long bus ride to the Berkshires, and because their personal trainer is obsessed with "hydration," and now they are buying designer water the way normal families buy juice packs. I take the shopping bag filled with Fiji bottles and try to wedge them into my already bursting backpack. Is there really a difference between Fiji and, say, Dasani? My mom swears there is. The only thing that I like better about Fiji is the way they decorate the bottles.

Charlene calls out all the other names on her long yellow pad and then we wait around for a girl who hasn't shown up and is already twenty minutes late.

I wonder why that is. They sent out the list of where to be and when about two months ago. It's not raining, it's not snowing, and it's a Sunday at eleven. What could possibly be keeping her? I look down at my watch as does about everybody else who's milling around, including adults who are dying to go out for Bloody Mary brunches once their kids are gone and kids who are dying to end this long good-bye.

Suddenly, as if to answer our prayers, a black Mercedes SUV screeches up and a girl who doesn't look to me as though she has to lose anything but some of the contents of her overstuffed Marc Jacobs bag gets out of the front seat and dashes up to us. Her mom doesn't bother to get out, just leans her head down and talks to us through the passenger-side window, apologizing profusely for being late.

"There's some kind of parade on 86th Street," she says, shaking her head in dismay. "It was bumper to bumper." Nobody knows what the hell she's talking about, because as far as we know this is one of the Sundays that, if you can imagine, nothing is going on in Manhattan. No Pulaski Day Parade, no St. Patrick's Day Parade, no Puerto Rican Day Parade, no Salute to Israel Day Parade, no Gay Pride Parade, nada.

"Maybe it all just looked like a parade to someone who comes from Scarsdale," I whisper to my mom. She smiles slightly, but doesn't reply. Scarsdale is an upscale part of Westchester County filled with high-achievers. The reason that I know that she comes from there is the bumper sticker on her car: MY DAUGHTER GOES TO SCARSDALE HIGH SCHOOL.

"You must be Carla," Charlene says. Carla smiles and nods. I can't help noticing the frosted-pink eye shadow that matches the icy-pink T-shirt that matches the frosted-pink toe polish that matches the pink tube of lip gloss hanging from a pink silk string around her neck. Very glamour-puss, if a touch excessive.

"All aboard," Charlene calls out. "Say your last good-byes." My mom gives me a tight hug and then looks me in the face. "Write to us every day and let us know how it's going," she says. "Have a great time, and remember—wear sunblock!"

Even though we're allowed to have cell phones (probably because there's no service anyway), the camp strongly discourages phone calls for at least the first two weeks and prefers snail mail. Something about phone calls getting in the way of us adjusting.

My dad is next, pulling me to him and holding me tight for a minute. "Have a great time," he says, his voice almost breaking. "I love you, don't forget that."

I nod and mutter something about loving him too. Finally, I turn and get on the bus, going almost all the way to the back so that I can watch the action in front of me. I slide in and take the seat next to the window.

Carla walks to the back too, and then hesitates as she gets to the seat next to mine. "Is it okay if I sit here?"

"Sure," I say, even though I'd rather sit alone and listen to the new Green Day CD that I just downloaded onto my iPod.

The bus is just about filled, and Charlene is busy counting heads to make sure that everybody she checked off has gotten on. After the final count, the bus slowly pulls away. A sea of parents start waving their arms madly at us. We wave back for a minute, and I see cell phones coming out of bags along with more iPods, *Cosmopolitan* magazines, chick-lit novels, and electronic games. I lean back and close my eyes, contemplating what my home in the Berkshires will be like for the next eight weeks or fifty-six days, or one thousand, three hundred and forty-four hours. . . .

THREE

I arrive at camp seminauseous from the bus ride and nearly starving. Almost three hours, and the "snack" was one medium-sized banana and a bottle of water. It's almost lunchtime, and after we're shown to our bunks, we'll get to eat our first meal at Camp Calliope, which some of the kids on the bus are already calling Camp Calipers because we know they'll be using those plierlike instruments that pinch your fat to measure ours.

But first we're shown the bunk, which looks like a giant plywood box with exposed ceiling rafters, open closets, an attached bathroom—thank God—and pathetic bunk beds with the kind of thin mattresses they use in prison cells. The upper beds are about a seven-foot climb, so I immediately throw my backpack on a bottom bunk to claim it and then brush off a gynormous dead wasp that I find on top of the mattress.

"God," I mutter, swiping it with my bag. Flash back to me settling down on my pillow-top mattress at home with the snow-white scalloped sheets and the down pillows, and I'm almost reduced to tears. Carla, who, it turns out, is in my bunk, climbs up the wooden ladder that's bolted to the side of my bunk bed and says, "I don't mind sleeping on the top." She hauls her bag up, but not before pausing to apply more lip gloss, which she has done about thirty times since we left Manhattan. I don't know what she's doing in this camp—maybe Neiman Marcus's princess camp was filled. It's obvious from the sideward glances she gets, that the other girls are wondering the same thing.

We have a counselor named Karen who seems all right—at least not as irritatingly cheery as Charlene—and she introduces herself to all of us. She's tall and serious-looking, with a long brown ponytail. I imagine her shopping for "green" paper towels and having an organic garden. I know that she plays the flute. She's got a small room, separate from ours, which is good news, because it means we won't be eyed 24/7. While we're hauling in our bags, Karen suggests that we take a break and spend a few minutes introducing ourselves to each other. She looks at me, so I start.

"Cam Phillips from Manhattan." Momentarily I think about following with some right-on remark about not wanting to be there and totally selling out, but hold off. Ditto for adding "being here truly sucks." When it's clear that I'm not going to give out any more information, Karen turns to the girl sitting on the bunk bed next to mine.

"I'm Bunny Young," says a very bleached blonde with a breathy baby voice, who I've noticed has brought along a collection of food and dining magazines. Is it my imagination, or does she resemble a younger Martha Stewart minus the Birkin bag?

"I'm from Philadelphia—one of the fattest cities in the country," she adds. Everyone laughs or snickers, and she goes on. "And this is my first summer at a camp like this." She ends with a shrug. In a flash, I envision her behind a kitchen counter baking pies, because she looks like Miss Homemaker.

"Well, great," Karen says, breaking in to ease our discomfort. She points to the next girl, who's tall, with big blue eyes and an easy smile. She's wearing two thick braids. I can't help noticing that despite the heat, she's got on very cool pink cowboy boots. I don't know why, but I like that.

"Faith Masters," she says, with a heavy Texas drawl, "from . . . well, y'all can tell." We all smile. "I'm determined to lose at least 25 pounds this summer, and that's why I'm here." It's obvious that everybody admires her for wasting no time owning up.

"Great," Karen says. "And I'm going to do whatever I can to help you get there." She points to Carla.

"Carla Valentine," she says in a delicate voice, and then doesn't say anything for a long time. We wait, curious to see what she's going to tell us about herself. She tosses back her platinum hair slightly. "And I used to weigh fifty pounds more than I do. . . ." she blurts out. We all stare in disbelief. She's about 5'10", and not more than 120 lbs. It's close to impossible to imagine.

"So . . ." she says, exhaling for emphasis. "I'm here to keep doing what I'm doing so that I can keep the weight off, because . . ." she says, staring hard off into the distance. Then she shakes her head and adds, in a rush, "It's such a damn struggle." With that, she bursts into tears, and all of us are momentarily shocked and don't know what to do except look everywhere but at her, and try in our pathetic ways not to make Carla feel even worse. Karen immediately goes over and hugs her.

"I know how hard it must be for you, and we're all here to support you." Carla takes the tissue that Karen rushes to put in her hand and blows her nose. No one says anything, but at that point I'm starting to like her more than I did when I saw her jump out of her Mercedes like a carefree fashion model who was late for a shoot. Karen keeps a supportive arm around Carla for another minute and then points to someone with long, stringy brown hair wearing a bloodred T-shirt and cargo shorts.

"I'm Summer," she says, head high and acting aloof as though she's trying to pretend she's some Hollywood film star. "And when I get home from camp, no one, and I mean, NO ONE is going to recognize me! It's going to be one big BEFORE," she says, holding up two fingers on each hand and making little quotation marks, "and AFTER." She ends with a smile that vanishes in a nanosecond.

"Okaaay," Bunny says, and we all start to laugh.

Lunch is in the mess hall, a building that's half the size of an airplane hangar. All around the top of the walls are camp flags that look like the campers stitched them out of swatches of fabric. I later find out that they're the flags made by the winning sports teams and that the camp has been in existence for almost forty years.

"So weight-loss camps are nothing new," the director says, giving us the tour. "It's just that now with fast food and more women working so that fewer meals are served at home, weight issues are greater than ever and more and more people have to relearn the way to eat to stay slim and healthy."

No one in the group says anything; we're just following him around like baby chicks. What I'm wondering is whether they've figured out how many calories you burn on the tour and if that's taken into account as part of the day's exercise, because I sure hope so. Right now, even with the dead wasp, the only thing that I want to do is sleep.

"Well, I've talked enough," Mel says, holding up his hands like a traffic cop. Mel is short for Melvin, and he's the owner of the camp along with his wife Lillian—who looks more like his mom, because she's one of those hold-out types who refuses to color her gray hair or have the bags fixed under her eyes.

We all head to the tables that our groups are assigned to and then get in line with our trays to pick up our food. I think there's a reason that we eat cafeteria style—we're forced to be separated from the food by a stainless steel barrier. I push the red plastic tray along and start loading it with an iceberg lettuce salad and a packet of gluey-looking low-fat Italian dressing, and then take a plate with oven-baked chicken (cornflake crust, I think) posing as

fried. To go with it there are dishes filled with whipped potatoes, each portion about the size of an A-cup, coleslaw
made with vinegar and probably artificial sweetener—
heaven forbid mayo—and string beans. Fresh strawberries
and vanilla wafers are dessert.

After lunch, we go back to the bunk and have a free period before heading to the dock for water safety tests that are
mandatory before they'll let us swim or go boating.

"Well, well, look what I found," says Summer, staring
into her backpack. "A Milky Way." She smiles seductively.
"Any takers?"

There's silence in the bunk as everyone instantly stops
writing letters or unpacking clothes. She looks at me with
her eyebrows raised.

"Cam?"

I pause for a minute and then shake my head. "No. I'm
more into Nutrageous."

"Bunny?"

She shakes her head.

"Carla?"

Carla makes a motion that indicates that she's throwing
up. We all laugh.

"Faith?"

The West Texas cowgirl just studies Summer. Then
slowly, she sits up in her top bunk bed and swings her

legs over to the ladder. She climbs down and walks over to her, hands on hips.

"Show it to me," she says, challengingly.

Summer reaches into her bag and acts like a magician, suddenly whipping out her fist and opening it. "Fooled ya," she says, showing us her empty hand and smiling widely. "I was just trying to find out who was the weak link."

FOUR

T his camp is a virtual Olympic village. You can kayak, row, swim, water-ski, rock-climb (uh-huh), hike, bike, do aerobics, yoga, weight training, etc., double etc., triple etc. I scan the list—unfortunately there's no thumb-sucking or butt-rocking. I get to pick at least three per day (so-called electives), not counting tennis, basketball, and softball. I go with hiking, rowing, and water aerobics. Hiking sounds easy. It's walking, right? What's hard about that?

"We'll start out with two or three leisurely miles," Fred, the hiking leader, says to us with a smile. "Who has hiked before?"

There are a few shoulder shrugs. Does hiking to the bunk count, because the hills in this place remind me of triple-black-diamond ski runs, not to mention the rocks and ruts and tree roots that you have to step over or around so that you don't actually kill yourself.

Was that what motivated them to build the camp here? I knew the Berkshires were mountains, but I didn't think we would be climbing them half a dozen times a day. So I lace up my brand-new L.L. Bean hiking boots (which add about ten pounds to my weight) and find that after about half a mile there's some little piece of something inside the left one that's gouging out a serious piece of skin. I suppose that Fred realizes that something's amiss after he hears a string of "shit" and then "shit" and then "shit" again as I try to tunnel down into the boot with my middle finger to get that little poking thingie away from my skin.

"Cam, what's the matter?" he asks. I point to my boot.

"The boot is doing surgery on my foot. I think I have to go back."

"New boots?"

I nod.

"Should have broken them in before you went hiking."

There aren't too many mountains in Manhattan, I'm tempted to say, but I don't. He reaches into his backpack and pulls out a roll of what he calls moleskin along with a pair of scissors and then motions for me to take off my boot. In the meantime everyone else takes advantage of the break and sits down to rest, mop sweat off their faces, and drink water. Fred cuts off a piece and covers the side of the boot with the patch and gives me a Band-Aid to cover my blister. Magically, the problem seems to be solved, and I keep on walking.

The problem with hiking, as I see it, is that the more you sweat, the more appealing you become to the bugs. I guess sweat is like Obsession to them, because the harder you work, the more they fly in your face and buzz around your ears like you're lunch. I'm counting my bites and thinking about mosquitos and diseases like West Nile and malaria—and hell, even ticks and Lyme disease—all the while trying to slap every flying thing away in a kind of one-TWO, one-TWO, one-TWO, one-TWO, one-TWO slap rhythm, or, as my lit teacher would see it, iambic pentameter bug swatting.

I don't have to bitch, because Bunny's doing enough for all of us. Clearly Miss Homemaker doesn't find hiking as easy as pie, because she's cursing in time to our footsteps, and instead of hearing *left, left, I left my wife and forty-eight kids home in the kitchen in starvin' condition with nothing but gingerbread left, left,* I hear *shit, shit, these bugs are like shit, shit. . . .*

Fred stops again. "Did you put on bug spray?"

"Negative. I hate that stuff," she says. "It smells like machine oil or something."

"It does the job," Fred says, in a clipped voice that tells me he was probably a marine. Now he reaches into another pocket of his backpack and pulls out a can of bug spray that sure doesn't look like something you'd find at Sephora. It's a serious green bottle—the kind they would issue you in the marines before you hit the jungle. I don't know what else he keeps in there, but I'm beginning to get the feeling that if they dropped Fred from a plane, wherever he landed he'd have the gear to survive, even if that meant having a scalpel to open someone's chest so he could massage their heart. Fred is just like that. I have no doubt that he has a degree in scouting or wilderness survival, if there is such a thing. Undoubtedly, he could find his way out of the bush with a compass, carefully nibbling on only the edible plants and avoiding the toxic.

People like me, on the other hand, always seem to leave home in a rush, forgetting something essential, like Tampax on day two. Tissues when I have a cold. Or an umbrella. I wing it, but Fred isn't the type who ever wings it. I just know that. After the next situation is in hand, we keep on going.

Even though I'm no Olympic athlete, I thought that I

wasn't really in terrible physical shape. I mean, like it or not, I have gym five times a week in school. We run, even lift weights. So why, now, do my lungs feel like hot burning coals, and why am I trying to suck as much oxygen as I can out of the sky?

"Just another half mile," Fred says, like the dentist who tells you halfway through a filling that he's almost done drilling. I look over at the other girls in my group to see if they're as hot and exhausted as I am. Carla seems to be fine, but I expected that. How could she have shaved off fifty pounds if she wasn't some kind of workout zealot? Summer's obviously in complete denial about how totally shitty she feels. The ice queen's chin is jutting up and out—end of story. She'll take whatever medicine there is to lose weight. Fortunately Bunny and Faith seem to be in my league.

"I know this isn't easy for some of you," Fred says, as if he's reading our minds, if not our faces. "But let me tell you that it gets easier the more you do it, and believe me, in a few weeks all of you will be enjoying the hikes, and you won't be huffing and puffing."

I give him a sidelong glance and don't say anything. Neither does anyone else.

"Is the way back downhill?" Bunny asks. Her face is covered with oily sweat, and I take comfort in the fact that I'm not the only one cocooned in perspiration.

"Yep," Fred says. "That's the cool-down."

"Can we go back to the bunk and rest after this?" I ask him.

He shrugs. "Depends. We usually schedule a few periods of activity before you have some down time."

I yank the pink index card out of my back pocket and stare at it. The ink is already bleeding, mostly from sweat. I look at the smudgy block letters and make out the word ROWING. Not only does that mean working my arms and back for *another* hour or more, it means walking half a mile to the boating dock. Down time? The way things were looking, for me the entire summer would be one long down time.

The only boating—if you want to call it that—that I was familiar with was:

1. Boating as in the Staten Island Ferry, which I rode a couple of times just for something different to do on a Sunday afternoon when my dad took me on a tour of lower Manhattan. We decided to see what our fair island looked like from the water, pretending à la one of his history lessons in disguise that we were immigrants sighting the good old U.S. for the first time.

2. Boating as in a rowboat in the Central Park lake where I went with my parents one Father's Day after

an eggs Benedict brunch at the Plaza Hotel when I was about ten. Of course, my dad and mom took turns rowing, while I sat back with my feet up and watched, occasionally sticking my toe in the water to test the temperature and to see if minnows would nibble on it. (They didn't.)

Now, though, I am about to do the kind of rowing that was popular on slave ships, assuming that I can manage to step into the boat without tipping it over. To his credit, Rick, the rowing counselor, doesn't laugh or make any of us feel like the pack of elephants we must appear to be. Once we're seated—two girls to a rowboat—we move on to learning how to hold the oars and then how to use them to get us from point A to point B. *So* fun.

What I didn't bargain for when I innocently signed up for rowing was an activity that I soon find out leaves a kind of residual paralysis not only in my arms and shoulders but also in my abs and legs. And I know that no matter how bad the ache is at this very moment, it will be worse tomorrow, never mind the blisters that will make my fingers resemble bubble paper.

"You know, I think I'd rather use the rowing machine in the gym," I mumble to Rick, attempting to row back to the shore. "I really can't do this," I hiss, feeling the needle of my tolerance meter starting to quiver wildly in the red, uncooperative zone. They can't force me to row—my father is a lawyer, I know what my rights are.

"C'mon, Cam," he calls out from his boat (which, miraculously, he keeps parallel to mine) at the sight of me struggling to keep the two oars working in tandem. "You have to give yourself a chance."

To Rick's credit, he seems like a tolerant guy who doesn't mind that he has to make two underwater dives to fish out the old, waterlogged oars that Bunny and Faith dropped to the bottom of the lake—on purpose, I think.

"Oh, my GOD!" Bunny yells as one goes down.

"Oh, mah GOD, mahn too!" Faith yells a second later. Rick dives under water to get them without a word.

"Cute ass," Bunny says as he disappears below the surface. Our laughter stops the minute he surfaces.

"You just have to get the hang of it," he says to me with a crooked smile as he cocks his head to the side and repeatedly presses his finger against his eardrum to get the water out. Getting the hang of it, I have to add, involves Rick eventually standing behind each and every one of us uncoordinated dorks, putting his hands over ours as he tries to demonstrate the strokes. No one objects to that part of the lesson. Can you guess why?

To put it plainly, Rick is insanely gorgeous. The camp directors weren't totally stupid: If their rowing counselor was some big, ugly whale with a hairy chest, every one of us would haul our butts out of the rowboats and head back to the bunks, swearing that we were going on strike. But no, Rick has dark curly hair and chestnut eyes, a warm, mellow voice, and a body so perfectly chiseled, he could model for Calvin. It was rumored that he had hooked up with Charlene. So IQ wasn't important to him. Still, it's hard not to get blindsided by his looks. But did my attraction help me get to the level of coordination, not to mention strength, needed to row for an entire hour after the hiking? Please. The effort is superhuman—an iron man kind of thing. WHAT-EVER.

Out of kindness, he cuts the hour short, telling us to row back to the side of the lake, parking the boats, where he will demonstrate the rowing technique once again. Fine with me. The muscles in my tongue are the only ones that haven't been strained.

"So how do y'all feel?" he asks, winking at Faith, when we finally trudge back to the grass.

"Like I'm dying," Bunny offers, rubbing her arms. "I don't think I'll be able to lift my fork at dinner."

"The food here doesn't weigh much," Faith says, examining her toenail polish. "It shouldn't be a problem."

"What about you, Summer?" Rick asks. "You've been pretty quiet."

"What about me—what?" Summer asks, acting as if she is oblivious to our complaining.

"Was the rowing hard for you?"

"For me?" Summer asks, giving Rick a withering look. "It was a piece of cake."

We all stare at her and then crack up laughing.

Never mind that we all go back to the bunk for free period and I fall into a coma instead of staying up and writing letters home. After an hour that passes in a heartbeat, I startle at the sound of Karen reading the headlines from *The Calliope Chronicle,* announcing that the following night we are going to have a social with the boys' camp.

I roll over and yawn. "I don't dance, so I'll probably skip it. . . . I mean what's the point?"

"The point, duh, is to have some fun," Bunny says. "I mean, I don't care if the boys here are fat and disgusting or whatever. I want to see if I can DJ, and anyway, I love to dance." In case I don't know what dancing is, she pantomimes the word *dance*.

"Mmm, I love to dance too, especially all by myself because there are no cool guys to dance with," Summer says with her usual icy sarcasm.

"Did anyone bring anything decent to wear?" Faith asks, taking the straw cowboy hat off the side of her bed and spinning it around on her finger.

Carla shrugs. "I have some Juicy skirts and tops, but nothing really great."

"You are so lucky you can wear that stuff," Bunny says, shaking her head. "I haven't bought anything decent in years. Everything I put on looks like . . ." she sticks out her tongue and gags.

"Uh, reality check," I say. "We're talking about a social with boys who came to this camp for the same reason we did. They're not going to look like Heath Ledger or anything. I mean, why do you care?"

"Maybe fat Heath Ledgers," Summer says.

Faith jumps down off her bed and balloons out her cheeks. She starts to strut with her thumbs hooked in her belt loops, pushing out her crotch. "Hey, girls," she says, trying to talk like a guy. "Gimme some."

"You are sooo gross," Carla says, bursting out laughing.

I slide out the suitcase that I kicked under my bed on day one and examine a few tops that I didn't unpack. Two halter tops (even though on me they don't look quite the way they do on the single-digit-sized Express model) and a lacy black camisole with a matching cardigan. At least the cardigan hides my upper arms.

I'd be the first one in line if someone came out with a range of clothes called "Camouflage," with different designs targeted to hide the particular part of the body that you hated most—upper arms, thighs, belly, ass, whatever, made of a miracle sucking-in fabric. I stare at the cardigan and then close the suitcase and slide it back under the bed with my foot. What were the chances that by mid August my clothes would look any better than they did now?

After we stop at the mess hall for fresh fruit and ice pops, we have a class called nutrition. The idea is obvious: Learn more about the foods you're eating so—in the words of the camp bulletin—you make "smarter choices."

Smarter? That never entered my thinking when I swung open the door of the fridge. Need. Gratification. Pleasure. Fulfillment. But none of *those* words show up in the camp bible. I'm smart, especially when it comes to calorie counts, but a lot of good it does me. Now if the SATs were about that . . .

It's just that as a rule, the lower-calorie and low-fat foods don't appeal to me much. I'm guided by my stomach more than my brain. The good news is that the nutrition class is in an air-conditioned room with chairs—a relatively bug-free zone—and we won't have to walk, run, hike, pedal, row, skip, or even move a muscle. It's enough to make me jump for joy.

I sit in front, next to Summer. Her hair is long and ratty. You don't have to be Sally Hershberger, hairdresser to the stars, to see that if it were trimmed and shaped and she lost the mousy color, never mind some weight, she'd look like a different person.

Summer has the kind of face that magazines love to use for their before and after pictures, the ones that make you think, H-E-L-L-O, didn't it occur to you before this to get a decent haircut or hit Sephora for some uh, makeup? And that, uh, bun? Exactly what were you thinking? Or forgive me, could you smile rather than stare into the camera as if you're posing for a mug shot?

In Summer's case I'm convinced it has occurred to her that she could look a whole lot better, because she's always walking around with magazines, studying the pictures as though she's trying to memorize them. The only explanation I can come up with is that her steely will somehow makes her determined to lose weight *before* she does anything to look better, as if she's punishing herself in the meantime for being fat.

Punishment, in fact, is the operative word for everyone in this place.

1. *We* punish ourselves for being fat.
2. *Our families* punish us for being fat.
3. *Friends* punish us for being fat.
4. *Strangers* punish us for being fat, either by dissing us with clichéd remarks (i.e., "fat pig") or simply pretending that we don't exist.

The irony is: What other group that's discriminated against is asked to change?

According to something that I read on the Internet, a fat camp is supposed to be a place where you not only lose weight but also are with other people who are like you so that you feel comfortable. I don't buy it. There are a few kids here who are seriously overweight—like over 300 pounds—and whether we admit it or not, none of us wants to look like them and we don't go out of our way to be their friends. It doesn't matter who they are inside, we fixate on their size, and first impressions die hard. Even among ourselves, I wouldn't use the word "comfortable." We know what we look like and what we weigh, but we're not okay with it, and being here doesn't make us comfortable, especially when it's time to be weighed in.

In our bunk, except for Carla, all of us have about the same amount to lose. Still, that doesn't make us the same.

I can't remember for sure when it first hit me that Summer has an iron will that makes her different. Maybe it was the day we had gym and she stayed after the class was over to keep running on the treadmill when she could have come back to the bunk and slept. Or maybe it was at lunch when, defying her appetite, she ate just one bite of chicken along with the salad and then left all the potatoes, what little there was of them. Or the time she was studying the picture of Gisele in a Victoria's Secret catalog and then got up to peer at her face in the mirror as though she was hoping either to see some resemblance or morph into her if she stared hard enough. We all want to lose weight, but she's driven, as if she's a contestant on a survival show competing for the top prize.

Does she look different already? It's only been a week, so maybe it's my imagination. Could be that she just wasn't hungry the time I saw her leave almost everything on her plate. In fact, the next day she finished all her food at breakfast and even asked Bunny if she could have the awful white stringy part of the scrambled egg that she left back. Bunny shrugged, and Summer took that as a yes.

I watched as she swiped it and then sat there, oddly, as if she were paying attention to the way it went down. Then she eyed the table like a hungry dog looking for crumbs.

SIX

Nutrition class. First thought on my mind:

Spare me the lectures about the totally incomprehensible Krebs cycle, or about the bomb calorimeter (I swear that's the name), the thing that burns food and tells you how many calories are in it. This is vaca-tion, *not* school.

Second thought: We've all graduated from kinder-garten, so please do not hold up those wooden blocks that our science teacher thought to use when making a point about the boring building blocks of protein, followed by a discussion of the two kinds of carbohydrates—simple and complex—and, of course, everybody's favorite part of the diet, fat.

Third thought: At all costs, avoid discussion of the food pyramid, including how much of the food groups we should eat each day. There is just no way any of that can be translated into useful information when I'm up at the counter of the pizza parlor, not to mention Benihana, thank you very much.

But the biggest joke of all in our nutrition classes at school? The plastic food models that look as though they belong in toy-sized pots on a child's plastic stove. Everyone in my class cracked up when they showed us what a portion of rice looked like and how much spaghetti equaled one serving. I mean, do you know anyone who eats just half a cup of spaghetti? Their idea of how much you should eat for dinner could fit into the palm of your hand.

None of us paid much attention to any of it at all, except for the time we had to guess how much fat there was in things like doughnuts, cakes, muffins, and frozen entrées. Then we had to go to the supermarket and read food labels to see how close we were. Needless to say, we underestimated. But cut out all the fatty stuff and what you're left with is cereal, fruits, and vegetables—hardly much of a diet. So we continued taking the high-fat road.

The camp's approach is more practical, I find out. We start out talking about fast foods, and good choices and bad ones. Susan, a college-age instructor, holds up a list. The headline items in the bad category are:

- Burger King Chicken Whopper sandwich—570 calories;
- McDonald's quarter-pounder with cheese—510 calories;
- Burger King original Whopper with cheese—430 calories;
- McDonald's filet of fish sandwich—a surprise at 400 calories.

So much for feeling virtuous when I went for the fast food fish instead of the beef. She talks about the hidden calories in fat— 160 for the mayo alone in the Chicken Whopper. So what do you do? "Turn a bad choice into a better one," says Susan. She suggests things like having them hold the mayo or cheese and tossing out half the bun.

Then she moves away from fast food and onto small, meaningful changes in the way you eat and "cheating," which now is seen as a good thing. What do I mean?

1. Saying yes to pie, but eating only the fruity filling and leaving back the crust because it's made with lard;

2. Eating only half a frank and filling the roll with extra sauerkraut;

3. Making meatloaf by using a third less meat and compensating by adding chopped vegetables.

At least she's not closing the door on eating things that are out there in the real world, so I start to pay closer attention.

"Before you prepare a meal, go grocery shopping, or go out to dinner, have a healthy snack such as a piece of fresh fruit to take the edge off your appetite, so that you're not starving, and sanity rules, says Susan. "Small changes add up to big losses of calories and eventually big losses of pounds over the course of weeks and months."

"Months?" Summer whispers in disbelief. "I don't have months."

"So go lipo," Bunny says, making a slurping noise.

"Anything that you want to share?" Susan asks, stopping in the middle of her sentence.

"No," Bunny chirps, looking up, all innocence.

"No," Summer parrots.

"That's all for today then," she says, "except for a short assignment. Before next class, put together a list of twenty-five ways to cheat and cut calories in your diet."

I'm thinking of things like substituting yogurt for sour

cream in recipes and drinking club soda mixed with fruit juice instead of soda, but obviously Summer's mind is elsewhere.

"Upchuck," she whispers to no one in particular. We all look at her strangely, and she bursts out laughing nervously. "Just kid-ding."

SEVEN

They aren't like the group discussions the camp runs every week with the guidance counselor where we talk about pseudopsychological things such as:

Do you think of food as offering emotional comfort?
What triggers your eating jags?
Or
What pleasurable activities could you substitute for eating?

These are our own rap sessions, spur of the moment, but always late at night, before bed, usually when we're sure that Karen is asleep. Faith really started it one night when instead of talking from bed after lights-out, which we usually do, she plopped down on the floor in the middle of the bunk with her flashlight beamed up at the ceiling. Bunny swung her legs off her bed and joined Faith. Then I did. Then Carla, and finally, Summer.

The way we sat there in a circle in semidarkness, knees almost touching, reminded me of a séance that I read about where a group got together and sat holding hands in a room with the lights out and only candles burning. A medium was there, and soon she had the group's attention when she insisted that the spirits of dead family members had entered the room and were with them. She told them things that the spirits of the dead were saying to her that made even the nonbelievers move to the edge of their seats, because the things she supposedly "heard" were private and no one except their dead relatives would have known them.

In our case, someone randomly starts talking about what's on her mind (camp confession, if you will), and then everybody else joins in. It seems easier to tell the truth about yourself and everyone else when you can't clearly see their faces.

There's no set topic. Whatever is bothering someone is tossed around, running the gamut from "Isn't that woman in the kitchen gross? I hate the idea of her touching my food" to "Do you think that Mel and his wife still do it?" to things about ourselves that we hate.

Maybe the whole defenses-down, honesty thing can be summed up in three words: low blood sugar. Add to that physical exhaustion. So we talk pretty much from the heart.

"Whose misery are we sharing tonight?" Summer asks.

Bunny sticks her tongue out at her and says, "I have something to say." She holds her arms open and waves her fingertips, as if to suggest that we should all move closer together.

"I'm glad I'm here this summer because people who aren't dieting all the time don't have a clue how we punish ourselves for being fat."

"How do you punish yourself?" Summer asks, drily.

"I never thought I'd tell anyone this," Bunny says. "But since I'm at an F.C." (shorthand for "Fat Camp"—because none of us want to use the "F" word). She shrugs. "I was in a restaurant a few months ago, at a table near some really hot guys." She pauses to hug her knees to her chest. "My girlfriend and I had just come from shopping and walking about a thousand miles around the mall, so we were totally starving. We didn't even have to look at the menu, we just ordered BLT clubs and fries. The guys were just sitting there, not talking, kind of glancing over at us from the corners of their eyes. When the waiter walked away, one of them leaned over to me. "Hey, baby," he said, "did you ever think about going on a diet?"

"No WAY!" Carla blurts out, pressing her hand over her mouth.

"His friends cracked up, and I just wanted to completely die," Bunny says, dropping her head. "But the worst thing is not just what he said, it's the way that the words stay in my head and haunt me. Instead of just dismissing it as a stupid, cruel remark, I keep using that memory over and over to beat myself up."

"Whoa, wait, what did you say back?" Summer asks, fixating on the guy, not the bigger picture. "Did you just let him get away with that?"

Bunny doesn't answer for a few seconds and sits staring at her toes. Finally, she looks up at Summer. "Actually I was vicious," she said. "I told him that I thought about dieting, but decided against it." She stops and licks her lips, and Summer is looking back at her, expectantly.

"He looked back at me without saying anything, not following. Then I added, 'Because if I dieted, my brain might get as small as your dick.' "

"Get OUT!" Summer says, clapping.

"Did you REALLY?" Carla asks, her jaw dropping.

"No," Bunny says, shaking her head. "But I should have."

We stop to collect our mail and then go to our bunks for a free period before dinner. Two thick white envelopes edged in navy, from my parents, and one pink envelope, Evie. Guess which I open first.

She's writing from tennis camp in Massachusetts. She's been there, what, ten days? She's already met someone whom she now has a crush on—*critically G*O*R*G*E*O*U*S*, Cam, and from Manhattan!* She's having a "fabulous time" and the place is "amazing." What she doesn't have to say is that HER camp has incredible food (one of the girls in her bunk is the daughter of a chef who owns a four-star Manhattan restaurant, so you can be sure that he checked out the cuisine). No slivers of skinless chicken from anorexic birds for them. No silver-dollar-sized hamburgers. The place is strictly top sirloin.

I imagine that it's really one big gastronomic free-for-all, especially since they play tennis all day and use up like a bazillion calories. Plenty of pancakes, waffles, quiche, and bacon for breakfast, thick sandwiches for lunch, and for dinner, pasta, filet mignons, fried chicken, whipped potatoes, Caesar salad, pie à la mode, fudge

brownies, s'mores. I tuck the letter back into the envelope, pretending that my mouth isn't watering, and open
the ones from my parents. Everything with them is fine,
fine, fine, they are working long hours, and exercising
every morning with a new trainer since their regular guy
is training for some hellish endurance test in Death Valley.
Is that supposed to make *me* feel better? They ask the
usual barrage of questions about me and camp.

*Have you made any close friends? How are the counselors?
What are the activities like? How's the food?*

At the end they slip in that they are going out to L.A. for a
week because my mother's latest book was bought by some big
director and it's going to be made into a movie. Just great. I'll be
missing a trip to a place that I am totally dying to visit. Instead
of spending my days seeing movie stars' homes and shopping
at the celebrities' favorite boutiques—like Fred Segal, or its only
rival, Kitson—I'm a slave in a camp where they deprive you of
your right to decent food and enough of it, including essentials
such as *buttered* popcorn, not the dry, air-popped that they
bagged and brought with them for us at the movies, not to
mention the embarrassing sour pickles on a stick.

I toss the letters aside and take out my stationery to answer Evie. But ten minutes go by and I'm still holding the
pen over the paper, unable to write. What the hell can I
tell her?

1. I haven't met anyone GORGEOUS. I haven't met any guys at all.

2. I'm not close to any of the girls in my bunk. One of them is probably a closet bulimic. Another, Carla, sometimes cries herself to sleep at night and has a makeup bag filled with prescription drugs and I'm wondering if she'll end up OD'ing on them.

3. There is a social tomorrow night and I don't want to go, and even if I do, I haven't a clue what I'll wear, since I have only crappy clothes that don't even look good. I take the pen and stick it through the paper, carving out an X. There are seven more weeks of camp to go with nothing to look forward to except semistarvation. I stick my stationery box into my cubby and leave the bunk. Outside I see Faith, who seems to be heading to dinner, so I catch up with her. My only consolation is that she looks as unhappy as I feel.

"If you had to pick just one thing that you miss from home, what would it be?" she asks.

"One thing?"

She nods. Did she mean something like my queen-sized bed, or the ice cream sandwiches (or in my parents' case, the teensie nondairy "Cuties") that are packed into the freezer? Hard question, and I don't know what she's getting at.

"Second Avenue Bagels," I say, finally. It's the local place that has the best whipped cream cheese with cinnamon and raisins. I always have it on a giant sesame bagel. "I don't know, everything. What do you miss?"

"My dog, Brandy," Faith says. "And my horse, Scout, and going riding when no one else is around and galloping and feeling completely free."

"Not food, huh?"

She considers that and then shakes her head back and forth. Unlike the rest of us, Faith flew to New York from West Texas, and on visiting day, her parents will be flying in—leaving the animals behind.

"We're all giving up a lot to be here," I say, trying to act supportive. "I hope it turns out to be worth it."

"Was it your idea?"

I shake my head. "What about you?"

"I read about the camp online," she says. "I already outgrew my size twelve jeans, and I didn't want to end up looking like my mother, who has been a sixteen ever since she became pregnant with me. She used to be thin, and before she was married she even won the Miss West Texas competition. But now she's just overweight and doesn't care. She can't even get up on a horse anymore." We get our food and sit down before anyone else.

"But it's hard," she says, shaking her head. "Sometimes I just feel it was a mistake to come. Maybe I should just get the hell out of here . . ."

"Do you think anyone ever has?"

"Has what?" Karen, our counselor asks, sitting down with us and looking up, expectantly.

I look at Faith and look away. "Has actually lost more weight than they expected to."

"Very often," she says. "It's all how hard you work." Then, as if she's reading our thoughts, she asks, "How are you both doing?"

I shrug. So does Faith.

"Did I ever tell you that I was a camper here for five summers before I started working here?" she asks, lifting a forkful of broiled flounder.

This surprises me. She isn't overweight at all. "Nooo," we say in unison.

"Yes, and I hated it at first. I hated the idea of being told what to eat, and I hated the idea of not eating all that I wanted. It wasn't easy, but you know what?"

"What?" we ask in unison.

"The summer here flies by, and by the end of it, it

doesn't seem as though any of it was hard at all." She's silent for a minute and looks off. "Do you know how it feels to look back at term papers that you wrote in school a year or two earlier?"

I nod.

"And do you remember thinking, 'I can't believe that I wrote that. It took so much work. How did I ever do it?' Well, that's sort of what this place is like. At the end of the summer you will have lost weight, and when you look back, you won't be able to remember how you managed to do that, because believe it or not, you're going to have fun here."

Faith and I exchange glances.

"Maybe," Faith says. I shrug and take a forkful of pasta primavera from the teacup. If only it had a few more tablespoons of cheese. . . . At that moment, Mel, the camp director, comes by and asks Karen if he can talk to her. She nods and gets up.

"You'll see," she says, leaving us alone together.

"Five summers?" Faith says, raising an eyebrow. "Can you imagine?"

"Till you get it right."

She looks at me and laughs. How many calories does laughing burn? I have to look that up.

EIGHT

No one in our bunk would admit to being excited, anxious, nervous, psyched, freaked out, or anything at all about the fact that they'll be putting us into a room for the first time with the boys' camp. It's only about a quarter of a mile down the road from ours, but it might as well be a foreign country, because we rarely see or hear anyone male, except for Mel, who's as old as my grandfather, and the male counselors.

Still, despite the fact that everyone is in denial, the air is so charged with excitement that it feels as though the bunk will ignite. Eyeliner pencils come out of nowhere, and so do lipsticks, and mini makeup trunks of eye shadows, lip glosses, nail polishes, and blush. Hair straighteners get pulled out of duffels like rabbits out of magicians' top hats, and instead of running shoes, Tevas, and Birks, we're all sitting on the floor trying on each other's glittery sandals and high-heeled mules. And speaking of the floor, it's now totally hidden, littered with serious mountains of reject clothes after everyone flings aside one outfit after another in disgust until they come up with something acceptable.

"Which one looks better?" Bunny asks no one in particular as she tries two different shoes with her final outfit, a black halter top and a black-and-white striped miniskirt.

"The sandals," Faith says, as she pulls a lock of hair away from her head and catches it inside a ceramic straightener. "Definitely."

"Oh, yeah," Carla says, agreeing.

"Does my ass look like, freakin' gy-normous?" Bunny asks, trying to see her back view in the small mirror over our cubbies by climbing up on the ladder of the bunk bed and swinging to the side.

"Guys like that," I say. "T & A."

"I have a lot more ass than tits," Bunny says.

Summer takes her Victoria's Secret catalog and flings it at Bunny, shouting, "Easy to fix."

Carla turns back to putting on a white velour skirt and

a matching hoodie over a red tube top. She's the only one who doesn't have to ask anyone how she looks. I mean, hello, a size six? She'd look perfect in just about anything. Only I honestly think that this fact passes her by. She doesn't see herself as a model, she sees herself as more of a fat kid hiding out temporarily in a thin body, a loaner. Obviously life has done a serious trip on her head to the point that she's blind to herself.

Summer glances over at Carla briefly with a small smile on her face and then turns back to putting pale pink polish on her fingernails and blowing on them, as if it will make a difference. I notice the black satin demi-push-up bra hanging over the side of her bed.

After almost everyone is dressed, I slide out my suitcase and take out the black camisole and cardigan. I didn't bring anything great to wear because I didn't have anything great. Why buy clothes when you don't have a life?

I go into a stall in the bathroom and change, passing the mirror without looking in it. I'm wearing my best-fitting jeans and Faith's gold high-heeled sandals. Luckily we're both a size nine. At least they're cool.

"Are you sure?"

"Wear them," she says. "I want to be able to dance." I don't bother with makeup, but as we're heading out, she turns to me and holds up her hand, like a traffic cop.

"Wait." She turns back to her bed then points to the edge. "Sit," she says in a voice she probably uses to command her dog. A pink lip gloss comes out of her makeup bag and she puts some on me, with an extra dab in the middle of my bottom lip. "We're going for *le* relaxed, bedroom look," she says, trying for a French accent. She stands back and assesses her work, then reaches for a dark brown pencil. My upper lid gets pulled taut and she lines my eye, close to the lashes. The bottom lash line is next. Then comes black mascara. Another step back, and then she approaches with a thick brush and dusts my cheeks with a tawny powder.

"Voilà." She holds up a mirror.

I look into it longer than I intended.

"Let's go, gorgeous." She laughs.

"Here goes nothing," I say, head higher now as I walk out behind her.

The rec room has been transformed into an almost believable-looking dance club thanks to black crepe paper covering the walls, a mirror ball hanging from the ceiling, colored strobe lights, and a music system that's way better than I would have imagined. A big metal bathtub with ice is on top of the bar, filled with bottled water and diet soda. The munchies are cut-up fruit and air-popped popcorn. Most of the bunks are already here.

"Coo-ool," Summer says, true to form. For once she's made a conscious effort to pull herself together. Her hair is washed and blown out so it looks long and silky, and she's wearing jeans with a low-cut black top that shows her cleavage. If she lost weight, would she lose it above the waist as well?

"What do you think?" Faith whispers in my ear.

"About?"

"Them," she says, punching my shoulder and raising her chin in the direction of a group of boys who are standing around laughing nervously like they're frat brothers. One of them has on pants that hang so low they look as though they'll slide off his ass. Never a favorite style of mine. Another has terminal acne. A third is blond, not bad-looking, but about twenty-five pounds over-weight. He obviously skipped sunblock—his face is salmon pink. There's an Asian guy in a Hawaiian shirt wearing one of those huge red felt Cat in the Hat top hats on his head that one of his friends keeps trying to pluck off. He finally does, running away with it, starting a game that was popular in kindergarten, complete with running, shouting, and pushing, that leaves all of them in stitches.

"I'm not falling in love, if that's what you mean. Most of them seem pretty infantile."

Faith laughs. "Screw it, dance with me."

"Sorry, Texas, you're not my type."

She pretends to be offended, and starts dancing by herself, as if she's oblivious to everyone around her. Bunny joins her, and that seems to break the ice so that everyone else drifts toward the dance floor whether or not they have a partner. Besides me, Summer is the only one in our bunk who stands along the wall as if she's a reporter, taking in everything around her.

The room is soon filled with a bajillion people dancing. A second later, the music gets—*whoosh*—turned up to the max. It's deafening now, impossible to talk unless you shout in someone's face. I think the floor is vibrating, or otherwise it's my blood cells. It feels as though my entire body is imprisoned inside one of those vibrating massage chairs.

Mel and his wife walk in and try to act cool. They start to dance the way I imagine they did in the 1940s, showing all of us what FUN! this is. I give Faith a look and pretend to barf. She doubles over with laughter.

Carla is dancing with a boy that I didn't see before. He's tall, with hair as pale and Nordic-looking as hers. Think Ralph Lauren ad, yachting motif, and a model who has let himself go. If he lost weight and firmed up, he would definitely be hot.

Bunny dances in circles by herself, checking out the crowd around her. When the music slows, she goes over and sits next to Rick, our rowing counselor, who is now the DJ. He looks as good in clothes as out of them. The black T-shirt seems to caress his six-pack.

Almost unconsciously, I make my way over to the popcorn. I reach out and grab a handful, then another. While I'm munching away though, I flash back to the phrase "Emotional Eating" that has come up now a few hundred times, and I ease away from the table so it doesn't look like I'm a poster girl for self-medicating with food while everyone else is normal enough to just be out there dancing. I work hard at looking casual, okay with being terminally on my own. I look for someone to hang out with, but, of course, no one comes up to me and asks me to dance. No one male, that is, so I'm back to feeling like I'm:

1. Totally invisible.
2. A complete nerd.
3. An alien from another planet who doesn't fit in any-where.

There is nowhere to hide in this room. It's warm—no, actually hot as a sauna, prickling my skin—and this whole attempt at a good time is starting to make me short of breath because the room is getting more and more packed, like one of those phone booths that they try to jam with as many people as possible. So right about now I begin to do my usual character assassination on myself:

- Is it my weight that's making me feel like a total misfit?
- Is it just me?
- Why don't I fit in?
- Exactly where should I put the blame for my total misery?

I end up parking myself in the corner with a bottle of Poland Spring in my hand, giving it a job. Sweat is beading on my forehead and the T-zone controller that I borrowed from Faith to prevent shine has done zip and I know without looking that my nose is probably shining like a 60-watt bulb. I press the cold bottle against my forehead while I watch Faith and then Summer, who is now dancing near her.

They're dancing alone. *They* don't seem embarrassed. Why can't I get up and dance by myself as if I don't care without feeling like a complete jerk?

I go outside to be alone and finally take a deep breath and feel some of the tension flowing out of me. It feels comfortable to be in the dark, not on view. I sit on the steps, staring up at the sky, trying to pick out the Big Dipper. The stars disappear in Manhattan. It's a black canvas with only moonlight and the tracery of skyscrapers. The small squares of light from apartment windows are like dots that don't connect to form a real picture.

The best place that I've ever watched the stars is the beach in Cape Cod. My parents and I spent a summer there in a house that we rented near the ocean. After great lobster dinners, we'd sit outside on the porch trying to pick out the constellations.

I once asked my father how the pictures got up in the sky and he laughed. The constellations were just images that people came up with to help them remember which stars were which out of a thousand or more that you could see on a clear night, he said. We talked about life on other planets, if there was such a thing or could be. Then all the sightings of unexplained flying saucers, or the ET-like pictures that people drew of so-called aliens that they claimed they had seen or been abducted by. There were too many accounts that were similar, my father said, shaking his head. It was comforting to go inside after that and fall asleep knowing that we were together, safe from the mysteries of the universe.

Now, though, my parents are in one place and I'm alone in another. Maybe they're watching an art film in SoHo or meeting friends for dinner at the latest trendy restaurant, talking about their upcoming trip to the coast. They're having grilled fish, giant mesclun salads, and, in a moment of weakness, a hand-carved wedge of bitter-sweet chocolate cake that they'll split between them, still managing to leave a few forkfuls back.

I turn when I become aware of soft guitar music coming from the other side of the porch. It startles me out of my thoughts. He's sitting on the floor, leaning against the railing. Tall, long legs, chunky body. His head is down over the strings, a dark mop of hair covering his forehead. Was he there the whole time? The music stops, then after a few seconds, starts again. He's singing softly, almost to himself. The song sounds sad. I can't make out the words.

I get up and walk over. He keeps playing, as though he doesn't see or hear me. But when the song is over, he looks up.

"Hey," he says, softly.

"You're good." I crouch down and look at him. He shrugs.

"Really. Have you been playing for a long time?"

"Since I was six," he says, starting another song.

I sit there and listen. "I never heard that before. Whose is it?"

"Mine." He continues to play.

"Wow," I say, almost involuntarily.

He looks up momentarily, almost surprised. After more playing, he looks again. "Don't you want to go back inside?"

"Do you want me to?"

"No," he says, almost flustered, "I just thought . . ." He shrugs, not finishing the sentence.

I gesture toward the door. "That's not really my thing."

"Gotcha."

I smile and he nods in agreement, continuing to play. Finally, he looks up at me, curious. "You gotta name?"

"Cam."

"Jesse." He pushes back the lock of curly hair that has fallen over his eye. It falls back down. "So what do you think of this place?" he asks, looking over at me.

I just shake my head back and forth.

"Touché," he says, holding my gaze and then looking back down at the guitar.

Shy, or just only interested in his music?

He plays another song and we sit without talking, my

eyes following his fingers as they move loosely, back and forth on the strings as though they are dancing.

"Ever play?"

I shake my head. "I took piano . . . but I hated practicing, so my parents stopped the lessons. I think they were relieved when they could get that humongous grand piano out of the living room. Wanna teach me?"

"I don't know, maybe." He keeps playing, and neither of us says anything for what seems like a long time.

"Are you in a band?" I want to break the silence.

"Not anymore. It fell apart after the drummer moved out of New York. Now I'm kind of doing my own thing."

"I'm always doing my own thing," I blurt out, surprising myself. He seems to quietly take in what I say while he plays, as though his fingers are making the music by themselves. We sit that way for awhile, until the noise from inside gets louder and some of the crowd pushes outside.

"Hey, Jesse, guitar man." It's a cackling male voice. "Play a song for me." That's followed by peals of laughter.

"You want to go someplace quieter?" he says, closing his eyes and shaking his head in mock despair.

"Where?"

"The tennis courts?"

We walk across a long field and enter the gate leading

to one of the courts. No one is around and we sit in the back, leaning up against the fence. Jesse glances up at the sky but doesn't say anything.

"Is this your first time here?"

He smirks. "Yeah, you?"

"Not my idea of the perfect summer."

"My dad was behind this one," he says.

"Why did you come if you didn't want to?"

"You don't know my dad," he says, making the guitar strings vibrate as if they were wailing.

"What about your mom?"

He shakes his head back and forth without answering.

Off in the distance there's a loud hooting noise, and I see the outline of two people at the end of the tennis courts. That's followed by someone doing a pathetic job of making bird calls.

Jesse looks up. "Assholes," he says, shaking his head.

"Are they in your bunk?"

"Probably . . . Aren't I lucky?"

I put my hands around my mouth, forming a megaphone, and make the same calls back. "So you just have to be a bigger one."

He smirks. "That's not hard." He puts the guitar down and grabs a tennis ball that's wedged under the fence and flings it toward them. I hear a thud as it hits.

"Fuck," a male voice says. "What was that?"

"Somebody threw something," the other one says. "I'm getting creeped out." Then it's quiet.

Jesse picks up his guitar and starts to sing softly, "See you later, alligator . . . In a while, crocodile. . . ." I laugh, and he reaches out his hand and messes my hair. I'm glad it's dark so he can't see me blush.

NINE

"**S**o what did y'all think of last night?" Faith asks to no one in particular as we're sitting around having breakfast.

"I literally danced my ass off," Bunny says, holding up her hands and shimmying her shoulders back and forth. "And I volunteered to DJ at the next social and Mel said yes, so I had a VERY cool time."

"I had fun too," Carla says, leaving it at that.

"What's the Viking's name?" Summer asks Carla.

"Trevor," she says, leaving it at that.

It didn't go unnoticed that Carla got more attention than anyone else. If her blond hair wasn't a boy magnet, her body certainly was. I even saw Rick looking at her.

"And what about *you*, Cammy," Summer says, picking us off, one by one. "I saw you hunkering down with that tall guitar player—kind of sexy, with those big bad shoulders."

"Well, it beat sweating like a pig on the dance floor," I say, flatly, staring back at her.

"Oh, I bet it did," she says, suggestively.

I give her back one of the withering looks that by now all of us have perfected thanks to watching the master.

"I think we should definitely get the day off from sports," Faith says, trying to come to my rescue by changing the subject. "I mean, didn't we do enough exercise to meet the daily requirement?"

"Ha," Bunny says. "Fat chance."

When Charlene walks by, the topic changes to the evening activity. She tells us that they're having a wardrobe consultant come to camp to talk about figure-flattering clothes. Clearly they're trying to work the problem from all angles.

"She's an image consultant who does a lot of work for fashion magazines," Charlene says, obviously bowled over by the thought of meeting a fashionista.

"She must be desperate for work if she's coming here," Faith says, after Charlene struts off. We all snicker.

"Wear your muumuus girls," Summer says, ballooning out her blouse. Bunny gives her a high-five.

As we walk down to the lake, Faith motions for me to come over to her. "So do you know who that guy was last night?"

"Jesse," I say, shrugging. "That's all he told me."

"Jesse *McKinley*," she says, as if that's supposed to mean something. I stare at her blankly.

"Duh, as in son of Jack McKinley?" Faith says.

I still look at her blankly.

"Cam, where have you been? He's just the coach of the country's top-placed basketball team."

Since I'm not a sports fan and could care less about that world, it means nothing to me. But Faith, who has three older brothers who are sports fanatics, assures me that Jesse's dad is on the A-list—a major celebrity.

"I'm surprised he didn't say anything," I say.

"He didn't say anything because he'd probably like to forget his dad and his star athletes," Summer says, lifting an eyebrow. We didn't realize that she had come up behind us. "He doesn't exactly look like the bulked-up players on the team."

So he wasn't muscled like a star athlete. I hadn't fixated on his body, really. It was his eyes, below the mop of hair, and what was behind them. Mostly, they were on his guitar, his safety net. But then when I wasn't expecting it, he'd look up searchingly, like a kid who was afraid to out-and-out stare, but wanted answers.

He wore a White Stripes T-shirt over jeans, ripped at the knee. He had to lose weight and firm up, but he was something like six-foot-four. I wonder—for his sake—if they feed him more than the measly portions they give us.

So Jesse's dad is some major-league celebrity. If I were home, I would have Googled him to see what came up. But I am laptopless here, waiting on the new one my parents agreed to buy me as part of the bribe to get me to go to camp, the unspoken words being *after you lose some weight*. That leaves the antiquated computer in the tech center that I have access to only during my free period.

But the schedule doesn't leave time for me to dwell on Jesse, his dad, or the boys' camp at all because our activities zap all energy, body and soul—clearly the point, so that we don't dwell on food or anything except working our butts off so that we drop to sleep in spite of the mosquitoes and lack of AC.

Not that my parents are sympathetic.

Dear Cam:

It sounds like the camp is trying to offer you a terrific athletic challenge—and believe me, we know that it has

*to be a hard adjustment for you, but we also know (since
you see how hard we ourselves work out and we're three
times your age!) that the effort pays off many times over.
You'll firm up, be more energetic, and overall just feel
better about yourself. And think about all the fun you
can have shopping for new clothes for school!*

*On other fronts, the house feels so empty without you.
Your mom and I have both been putting in lots of hours
at work but trying to take in some movies and plays in
the evening. We talk about you all the time and can't
wait to see you on visiting day. Can't believe that it's just
two weeks away.*

All our love,
Dad

And unlike Evie, who gets care packages of Godiva
chocolates and things like chocolate turtles, what do I
unearth in my care package that's wrapped with fancy
French toile paper with gorgeous blue ribbon? Would you
believe:

1. A small battery-operated plastic fan
2. Avon Skin So Soft
3. Two crossword puzzle books
4. A bottle of pink Hard Candy nail polish

5. A lip gloss on a key chain.
6. Two rolls of stickers that say things like "Have a nice day!"

Whoopee!

So just two weeks until visiting day. Am I supposed to be excited? I miss them, but so far, I feel as though the amount of weight I've lost is anything but earth-shattering. They'll come out of their car, looking for me, only to see me from a distance and be instantly disappointed. They'll exchange knowing looks. *She hasn't changed very much. The camp isn't working. This is what we spent thousands of dollars for?*

Or worse, they'll see that I just wasn't losing as much as some of the other girls. *Is it her metabolism? Laziness? What's wrong with her?* They'll assume that it is somehow my fault. They'll think that I'm sneaking candy or not exercising hard enough. Not that I hadn't done some secret candy eating in the past, when I was home and supposedly dieting. Not that I hadn't gone to Dunkin' Donuts to hang out when I said that I was staying late at school.

Once they caught me, but that was a long time ago and we didn't talk about it anymore. Still, I knew they remembered. I'd see a glint in my mother's eyes the moment I looked at her that would tell me what she was thinking.

It's not as though I'm desperate to please them, it's just that after all I'm putting myself through here, I feel I should have more to show for it. I know the feeling—I've been there before. Of course at home, the diet plateau would be followed by a secret visit to the refrigerator for some fab dessert—my consolation prize. Or I'd swing by the grocery store and buy chocolate chip cookies that I'd hide in my backpack.

Here there's no refrigerator to go to—just the point. (Rumor has it that one of the kitchen staff has set up a side business selling candy to any camper desperate enough to pay five dollars a bar, but I haven't checked it out, and as far as I know, neither has anyone in my bunk.)

I think of the nutrition class. *Small* changes? I've said good-bye to E. J.'s cheeseburgers, sweet potato fries, milk shakes, ice cream, decent granola, smoked salmon, bagels, and the list goes on. And what good has it done me? Next nutrition class, I stick up my hand.

"I've given up three quarters of the foods that I eat at home and I'm working out like a pig, so why haven't I lost more than seven pounds?"

Susan nods as though she's been asked the question before. "Whether we like it or not, our bodies are looking out for us," she says. "They protect us against losing too quickly. Yes, there's an initial and impressive loss, largely of water, when you start eating less, and especially when you start cutting back on carbs and eating a more high-protein diet, but then the weight loss levels off slightly."

"Oh, great."

"You keep losing, but it's a slow and steady loss," she says. "Because if you starved, it would be too traumatic to your body, and the shock of the sudden drop would be worse than staying at your heavier weight." She goes on about how smart the body is, and how sensitive an instrument, but somewhere along the way all I keep thinking about is how the summer is only eight weeks long and that it had better damn well pay off. Everyone around me seems to be doing better than I am, but I don't want to bring that up in class because it will look like I'm jealous and resent their success.

Susan pulls me aside as we're all filing out of the room. "Don't be discouraged, Cam," she says. "Your weight loss is right on target, and believe me, if you lose it slowly and steadily, you'll have a much better chance of keeping it off."

"Everyone else seems to be losing more than I am," I say, surprised that it comes out in a desperate whisper.

"No two bodies work the same way," she says, touching my arm. "But that doesn't mean you won't be successful. In fact, maybe you'll have an easier time keeping it off. You have to be patient."

"Thanks," I say, more deflated than elated. "Whatever." I head toward the lake for rowing. Faith walks with me. She looks around and waits until Bunny is ahead of us.

"Get this," she whispers. "When the mail arrived yesterday, you know what Bunny got?"

"I give up."

"Three large Hershey bars."

"I thought they checked your packages."

"They do," she says, "but hers were hidden inside a set of Pottery Barn sheets. Do you believe it?"

"Skeevy."

"Really," Faith says.

"So let's raid her stash."

"I doubt there's anything left to raid," Faith says. "I saw her go into the bathroom, and it took awhile for her to come out."

"Pathetic."

"Totally."

Just then Charlene catches up with us. "So is any of this getting any easier?" I glance at Faith.

"It's bearable," Faith says, obviously anxious to avoid any soul-searching with Charlene. I nod in agreement.

"Well, I have a new activity that will burn fewer calories but will offer a different kind of challenge, and we need your help."

We both look at her warily.

"We're looking for some new recruits for the staff of the camp newspaper," she says. "Are you girls game?"

"Sure," I say, a little too readily. Unless you had to work on the paper while swimming the lake, it was something that I wouldn't mind doing. Faith is suddenly mute, so I punch her arm.

"Not *moi*," she says, finally. "I can barely spell."

"Well, then, Cam, it's you," she says, in her usual cheery voice. "You come from a writing family. You're our new editor in chief—CONGRATULATIONS!" She high-fives me, pivots, and struts off, tossing her blond mane over her shoulder.

"Waaaiiit," I shout after her, but by then she's already far ahead of us and can't or doesn't want to hear me ask her if I can—maybe—think about it.

TEN

Cam, best friend:

So how come all I've gotten from you are like two measly letters and I've sent you—what—at least six or seven zillion????? Do you need stamps? Are you really there or have you run away? Just kidding. I know that you're probably working your butt off and that you'll come home so gorgeous that everyone will freak.

Things here are still super. My fab guy (Seth) spends like every free minute with me and everyone teases me about how the two of us are joined at the hip. It's so amazing. I never thought that anything would happen this summer other than my serve getting better along with my game. Now I really know what LOVE means. HA! Write, dammit! Can't wait to see you in August!

   Love, Evie

I was hoping Evie would fail to notice that I wasn't writing her the number of letters that I swore on my life to send. The truth is every time I start one, I end up tearing it up. When your best friend is having the time of her life and you aren't, what can you say? You're totally thrilled that things for her are so totally kick-ass, never mind that your summer is a near disaster? I don't want to sound depressed and bitter and unable to feel happy for her, so I decide that it's better to let her think I'm too busy to write more than a quick, sketchy note.

But now, never mind writing to Evie, I'm getting ready to do another kind of writing. I'm in the camp newspaper office staring at the computer screen. All around me are the favorite recipes of the counselors and campers along with paragraphs from everyone with the heading THE BEST DIETING ADVICE I EVER GOT. I glance at them:

Brush your teeth after you finish dinner to get rid of the taste of food. If you're like me, you won't eat again because you'll be too lazy to brush again.

Put leftovers in the freezer—immediately. That way you can't go back for seconds.

Aside from regular food and diet stories, I want to write something a little out of the ordinary. Genes from my mother? Maybe. I briefly consider a kind of diet blog, but no, that's too personal and I'm not ready to print my innermost thoughts for everyone around me.

One of the counselors suggested a story about self-image, but I'm coming up dry until I start to think about a conversation I had with my shrink a couple of years back.

"So how do you feel about the way you look?" she asked.

The way I look? I gave her a blank stare. I had never really asked myself. Not that I had any illusions about who I was or could be, even if I lost weight.

Really, I never stare into the mirror the way girls like Summer and Carla do, as if they're addicted to looking at themselves and fascinated by their potential. I'm not totally weird-looking or anything. I may be fat, but no one has ever called me ugly. No, I don't have legs that are ten feet long, or sculpted arms. But my skin is pretty good—thank God I never had more than a few zits. My eyes are a decent, clear blue, and my nose is about the right size. It's just something about the width of my face and the fullness, I guess. There are no perfect planes or angles. No

sharpness to my chin, the kind of lines that make someone ask you to model in profile.

Not that I didn't try at one point or another to change
the shape of my face. I experimented with blusher and all
of the other things that those how-to makeup books de-
scribe to create shadows and hollows to thin your face. In
my case, though, nothing changed much except that
when I used all the dark powders to create shadows and
then put on dark lipstick to add more "drama," I looked
like a slut.

So what was my answer to my shrink? "I'm okay, I
guess." Shoulder shrug. "Could be better." Major silence.

"Better? Better how?"

"It's obvious, isn't it?" I said, testily. Was she blind?
Couldn't she see that I was overweight and that the reading on the scale was my first problem? If it wasn't for my
weight, I wouldn't be visiting her on Park Avenue twice a
week, taking up room on her overstuffed couch with the
tissue box inches from my hand.

But she didn't let it stop there. She wanted me to come
to terms with what I was feeling about myself, except that
I couldn't. I stopped thinking about my looks and even
stopped looking into mirrors. Instead, I started focusing
on things like drawing while watching MTV, and getting
decent grades in English and history. The letter A proved

that there were things in the world that I could try for and actually be successful at, in spite of failing grades on the scale.

So unlike Faith and Bunny, who strut around head high as though they were just named class valedictorians, I went the other way when it came to my body and jumped on the "I don't give a shit" bandwagon. It seemed pointless to turn myself inside out to try to look like what I couldn't, so why even wear makeup or buy decent clothes?

But after that shrink session, almost out of curiosity, I remember going through some old *Seventeen* and *YM* magazines where they have these quizzes made up of what look, at first, like totally unrelated questions, but when you add up your score, you are left with a profile of your type:

> You're a natural beauty, comfortable with yourself, uncomfortable hiding behind lots of makeup or frilly clothes. You like natural fibers, loose, comfortable clothes. You may be a vegetarian, or thinking of becoming one.
> **Or,**
> You're naturally sexy and outgoing. You

feel good in short skirts and high heels, or
even (why not?) going topless on the beach.
You like long, dangly earrings, you love to
line your eyes with black liner and wear shim-
mering eye shadow, even dusting some in
your cleavage. If he doesn't ask you out,
you're comfortable calling him and asking
him to dinner. Hot night out on the town?
You'd rather have a hot night in.

Obviously I didn't fall into the "sexy and outgoing" category. I think I came out a cross between "natural" and
"conservative." Evie ended up in the category that com-
bined a little of each: an eclectic type, or however they de-
scribe the person who's a walking identity crisis and can't
seem to make up her mind who she is, ending up with a
jumble of answers that fall into every one of the stupid
categories.

To turn up the heat, Evie and I went to Sephora, where
we each spent about a year's worth of babysitting money
on makeup so that we could make ourselves over.

"Clean slate," as she put it. "Our faces are our blank
canvases," she intoned like the high priestess of beauty.
However, when we came out of the bedroom with our
"canvases," heavily painted with the new fall colors ap-

plied as thick as oil paint, my dad, who was sitting in the living room reading the newspaper, almost dropped it.

"Going to a costume party?" he asked, looking mildly shocked.

We ignored him and immediately went out the door and down in the elevator to see what my new (and cute) doorman would say, but he was busy helping an old, bent-over woman get out of a taxi, and we didn't want to stand there forever like complete jerks waiting for him to notice us.

Instead, we went to Evie's house and continued the makeover by highlighting our hair—never mind that my mother almost went ballistic when she saw what I did and found out that the color definitely wasn't from the wash-out color that came in the spray can, left over from Halloween. (I mean, what were we to do? We were old enough to know that the old "put lemon juice on your hair and go sit in the sun" advice is totally bogus and probably came from someone who was bribed by someone else's parents.)

Of course that was then and this was now, two weeks after I met Faith with her Trish McEvoy makeup brushes, a birthday gift from her aunt in New York who works for *Allure* and gets lots of freebies. Faith opened my eyes up to the fact that, well, at least I could look better than I did.

And that opened up a lot of possibilities in terms of experimenting with makeup and actually improving my mood in spite of my weight.

Now that I've started to study myself in the mirror, and seem to continue doing it (maybe it's a bug I caught in the bunk), I'm starting to realize that dissing makeup altogether was a real mistake. Even if I'm not losing as much weight as I want to, makeup definitely helps me look more alive. And since Faith opened up her makeup case and offered "anything you want," I took the Nars blusher, the Cargo eye shadow, the Lancôme eye pencil, and some pale-pink lip gloss that she swears makes me look "SO COOL."

So now, here I am, editor in chief of the *Calliope Chronicle,* total circulation maybe 180, and out of sheer boredom, I decide to goof on everybody by coming up with a quiz to help you figure out what you really think about your body.

Oh, and did I mention that I'm not the only new recruit on the staff? Forgive the oversight. The new managing editor—as of yesterday—is Jesse McKinley, who immediately saw the job as a way cooler thing to do than going to wood shop to make "dumb-ass model airplanes," as he says, or "learning to prepare crapola fillet of sole Veracruz in cooking class." So Jesse and I are sitting around with our feet propped up on the desks, talking about what kind of questions we would put into the quiz.

"Is your fat ass a source of deep embarrassment?" Jesse asks, in a mock-serious tone. "Do you require two seats on an airplane instead of one?"

"Noоо," I say, smirking. "It's got to sound like something out of *YM* or *Cosmo*."

"Like?"

"Like . . . You're at a rodeo bar and trying out the mechanical bull, but by the time you're bucking up and down, you realize that you're wearing your lowest-rise jeans and they're now around your hips so that you bare butt is peeking out and all that's between you and your Calvins is a thong that offers as much coverage as a shoelace. Do you:

a. Turn completely magenta and go hide in the bathroom the very second the ride ends.
b. Hold on tight and have a good laugh while the world stares at your buns.
c. Laugh it off and tell everyone you were wasted out of your mind and didn't know what you were doing in the first place.

"I get it," Jesse says. "So what would you do?"

"Probably all three." I turn back to the computer to continue. We both sit there staring at our screens for inspiration. Jesse starts typing and so do I, but we don't say anything to each other. A few minutes later he swivels around in his chair.

"You have a date with the girl/boy of your dreams, but everything you put on makes you look fat and feel miserable. Do you:

a. Call to say you've come down with the flu and have to cancel.
b. Dress all in black because it makes you look slimmer.
c. Put on the most outrageous outfit you can think of no matter how it makes you look and go out and PARTY with your date because it's Saturday night and man, you just don't care.

"Good. So which would you do?"

"Probably cancel," Jesse says, with a half-laugh. "What about you?"

"I've never—" Embarrassing silence.

"Never what?" he says, eyes fixed on mine.

I take a deep breath. *Should I?* "I've never had a date

with the boy of my dreams," I say. There, I admit it. And now I know that I will turn magenta, so I swivel back to the computer, but can't resist glancing back at him. He's still staring.

"What?" I say. He looks away for a minute, and then back at me.

"I've never had a date with . . . with . . . the girl of my dreams."

"Really?"

"My life's screwed up," he says, his hand rubbing the back of his neck.

"Maybe it's not just you—"

"Yeah, it is," he insists, in a rush.

I'm not sure what he wants to tell me, or how much he wants me to know. And I don't even know if I want to know, at least not yet. I turn back to the computer and start typing again. Then I glance back at him. He's still staring.

ELEVEN

For the first time it's Carla who sits down on the floor in the dark with her flashlight aimed at the ceiling, her way of telling the rest of us that we should join her.

"You guys are like my sisters. . . . And that really means a lot to me," she says, when everyone else has formed the circle. We wait for her to go on. Ever since her outburst the first day, I'd changed the way I felt about Carla. There is no way I can resent her, despite the fact that she's thin and has this ethereal beauty. She's the pathetic puppy in the bunk and she seems to bring out my protective instincts, as if she won't survive if all of us don't treat her with special care.

Nothing about Carla is laid-back, easy, or confident.

Everything about her seems tentative and vulnerable. She's living on the edge, as if she feels that she doesn't have as much right as anyone else to exist. When we eat together, I can see her love–hate relationship with every bite of food, whether it's on her own fork or somebody else's. And it isn't only me who sees it.

"Even though you are like *so* disgustingly thin," Bunny jokes, "I'm glad to be here for you. I know how hard you are on yourself," she says, turning serious, "and sometimes, I still feel sorry for you."

"I know what you mean," Faith says. "You're really tough on yourself, Carla."

"I . . . I didn't know that it shows," Carla says, haltingly.

"We hear you cry at night, sometimes," I add, without thinking. Maybe I shouldn't have said that.

"I can't help it," Carla says. "All I think about is my weight and—"

"You've got to cut yourself some slack or you're going to explode," Bunny says. "Food isn't a drug—you can't stop eating."

Faith looks at Bunny and doesn't say anything.

"I know how Carla feels," I say. "The whole world sees the ideal woman as being thin and everybody else who isn't as butt-ugly and repulsive, so it's easy to brainwash yourself into thinking that your only goal in life is to stay thin, so that's all you think about."

"So what's wrong with that?" Summer asks. "What are we supposed to be thinking about? Who's going to be running for president and whether the world's coming to an end? You have to be single-minded when you want something, especially when you're fighting nature and refuse to let it win."

"If you see it that way, then you're going to lose," I tell her, but she doesn't want to hear that.

"Well, we'll just see about that," Summer says, "because unlike the rest of you, I don't plan on shopping online for workout clothes at Zaftique.com for the rest of my life."

God, she is such a bitch. I glare right back at her, but don't want to start a fight, especially since this is about Carla, not us.

"You see how depressing this is," Carla cries. She jumps up and runs to her cubby. I hear her pick up a plastic bottle of pills and shake it. The next thing I see is her throwing something back into her throat, dry. "I take these stupid pills," she says, throwing the bottle on the floor. "Not that they do anything."

I'm getting an uneasy feeling now and don't know what to say. Maybe Carla needs her shrink, not us. "It's hard," I say, for lack of something else. "But don't punish yourself. At least you've lost the weight, and you're a babe, Carla, whether you realize it or not. You have to keep thoughts like that in your head."

Faith chimes in. "Cam's right. Half the boys—dorky or not—were staring at you the other night. And they weren't thinking about how much you weighed. It's something about you."

"No one has ever said anything like that to me," she says, different now, as though we were validating her. "Thank you, really. I . . . I just never think anything positive about myself. I feel like a fraud. No matter what the scale says, all I think is that I still feel fat, that the weight's still there and that it's going to get worse if I'm not watching out." She turns her flashlight upside down. "Whenever something goes wrong in my life, I blame it on my body," she says in a rush. "If I were different, if I could just eat like everybody else and not have this problem, this stupid ISSUE, but it never goes away."

"There's something I read once about protecting yourself from what bothers you," Faith says. Now she's got our attention. "A woman who was diagnosed with cancer was facing chemotherapy," she says, "and she was very afraid. So the way she got through it was by doing what she always did when she was afraid."

"Running away?" Summer says, drily.

"No," Faith says, shaking her head dismissively. "She pretended to slip her arms through a heavy white protective coat that she thought of as her body armor. When she had on the coat, she was shielded from whatever in life could harm her."

"That's so cool," Bunny says.

"I know, so Carla, maybe you need to think of something like that."

Carla crosses her arms over her chest and hugs herself as if she's trying it out. "Thanks."

No one says anything else, and almost simultaneously we shut off our flashlights and go into bed. I sense that something is different but at first I can't figure out what it is. Then I realize what I'm hearing—the quiet. Carla isn't crying.

TWELVE

If it isn't sucky enough that my parents are going to L.A. without me because my mom's book is being turned into a movie, their last letter tells me that some big-time Hollywood director has asked her to write the screenplay. So guess what that means?

> I'm really upset, Cam, because the director is heading to Japan to film another movie and he'll only be available to meet with us on parents' visiting day! Daddy's quite upset too, because I need him to come along and help work out the details of the contract before I agree to anything. I've asked the camp if we can visit the following weekend, and they said that it wouldn't be a problem.

We're just so sorry to disappoint you (and ourselves!),
but I hope that you'll understand how big a career move
this is for me. We'll call you soon.
   All my love,
   Mom

I tear the letter into postage-stamp-size pieces, and do
the same to the one that I'm about to mail them. Fine.
Don't come. I don't care if I never see them for the rest of
my entire life. If her stupid book is more important to
them than coming to see me for one day, six pathetic
hours, when everyone else's parents will be racing up
here, then they can fly to L.A. and stay there. I'll sign up
for boarding school and go directly from camp without
going home.

At least my parents have their priorities straight: My
mom's career comes way before visiting her only child. I
run from the bunk, off in the direction of the newspaper
office. It's usually empty—Jesse inevitably shows up late
because his softball game always goes into extra innings.

I yank open the screen door, and collide with him
going out.

"Shit," I yell, slamming my face into his chest.

"Hey, what's the matter?" He grabs my shoulders.

"Nothing . . . What are you doing here?"

"I left softball; I pulled a muscle."

I turn and stalk off, going back toward the bunk.

"Hold it," he says, running after me and grabbing my arm. "What's wrong?" he asks, breathlessly. "Did I screw up?"

"Please." I push his hand away. "Just leave me alone now." My messed-up family life is not his business or anyone else's. I run and then finally stop and walk until I get to the far end of the baseball field. There's an old leafy tree just behind the outfield and I sit down, pulling out the letter from Evie.

> *So Cam, you won't believe this. Seth and I are like so hooked-up. He gave me the gold ring that he got from his parents for his sixteenth birthday, and I wear it on a chain around my neck. He's an unbelievable kisser (dry, not sloppy and wet) and, well, more about that when I see you.*
>
> *Camp is great but your presence is missed like crazy. The girls here are so competitive, and even though I'm a pretty decent player, I'm really not in the same league as some of them, and anyway, there's no way I'll ever end up like Sharapova, but whatever. I tried to call you on my cell, but, of course, there's no service here. What did I expect? Tell me more about Jesse. I never heard of his*

father either, but I asked some of the girls in the bunk if
they did, and one of them said that her brother has a
book that Jesse's father wrote on the psychology of win-
ning because he's supposed to be unbelievable at getting
players to do their best. (So does that mean we're guar-
anteed VIP seats at the Garden? Just kidding.)

   Write immediately and tell all.

   Love, Evie

I stare at the pale-pink stationery with the scalloped
border and Evie's initials in maroon ink, the exact color of
Chanel Vamp polish: EAK for Evie Ann Kelly—across the
top. In her bubble of happiness, it is pathetically obvious
to me that she has no clue whatsoever as to what I am
going through. It's not that I *didn't* want things to be going
well for her, it was just that I had hoped she wouldn't be
so blinded by her own happiness that she'd miss—or ignore—the fact that for her supposed best friend, things
weren't quite so amazing or unbelievable.

Sometimes I honestly don't know whether to hate Evie
or love her for her total blindness. She never dwells on
my weight or feels sorry for me. In fact, she's so nonjudg-
mental that she probably forgot what kind of stink-hole
camp I was stuck in.

And Jesse, my fellow partner in misery? Why do I always start feeling guilty about things that I say or do? He has his own problems, but he doesn't complain—at least to me—about them. He's lucky: His music is his safe house.

What would it be like to have a father who was a celebrity who spent more time away from home with his team than his own child? My father travels for business sometimes, and we don't always get along, but he's always there for me. Jesse's dad has a reputation for motivating his team to win, so it makes me wonder if he's as good with his own son.

I head back to my bunk and drop Evie's letter inside my suitcase, grab sunblock and then throw it down, and go to the lake. It's almost time for rowing, and for the first time, I look forward to it. At least it'll help me get out some of my aggressions. No one else is around—they're all probably down there, ahead of me.

As usual, I walk without watching where I'm going, and I almost fall on my face after I trip on a chunk of tree root that's sticking out of the ground.

"Shit," I mutter, leaning over to rub the side of my toe. That's when I hear the strange sound. I look around, not sure where it came from. It's like the cry of someone who's sick or in pain, but I don't see anything, so I walk to another bunk and search around it. Still nothing. But then I hear it again and think that it's coming from behind the tree, so I walk toward it and spot the back of a girl's head. The hair is long, stringy. She's leaning against the tree for support with her head hanging down. At first I assume that she must have dropped something and is looking for it, but as I get closer, I see she has her finger down her throat. Then it occurs to me. What I heard was the sound of Summer forcing herself to throw up.

THIRTEEN

Spare me the talk about endorphin highs or being in the zone or whatever is supposed to happen to you when you're exercising hard and at the top of your game. Yours truly is nowhere near Nirvana. I haven't risen up, been reborn, or whatever. Still, I've gotten to the point where I can get through an hour of rowing without stopping every few minutes and glaring at Rick as though my misery is totally his fault. Ten days to parents' visiting day, but who's counting? I think about my parents and then try to:

1. Stop thinking about them staying at a hotel in L.A. that sends a Rolls-Royce to the airport to pick you up.

2. Stop thinking about them having dinner at celebrity-packed restaurants where chances were better than good that they'd rub shoulders with hotties like Chad Michael Murray or Ashton Kutcher while I am sitting ass to ass with fat girls. That's fair, right?

To make it worse, I'll be alone on visiting day when everyone else is with their families, and the following week when everyone is on their own again, I'll be saddled with my parents, and we'll be sauntering around the camp together beaming out the message:

D-Y-S-F-U-N-C-T-I-O-N-A-L F-A-M-I-L-Y

while everyone else is purposefully going to their activities.

My parents aren't stupid. They know very well that I'm furious with them because I stopped answering their letters. Finally they called Mel and asked—no, actually, demanded—permission to speak with me right then, even though that generally isn't allowed unless the phone appointment is set up in advance. So it's ten o'clock at night, and I'm already in my Victoria's Secret PINK nightshirt, getting into my bed, when I am summoned and have to drag ass to the phone.

And how does the conversation go?

"Cam, dear, I hope you understand that we tried to change the appointment over and over but there was no way that the director could do it."

Silence.

"We'll be there the following weekend. In fact, we're staying over at a hotel the night before so that we can be there at the exact stroke of ten in the morning."

More silence.

"Cam?"

"What?"

"It's one day. And we're sorry. What do you want us to do?"

"Nothing, Mother. Enjoy your trip."

I walk back to the bunk. Everyone else is sitting on the floor with their flashlights turned on. I join the circle and add my yellow pool of light to the ceiling, the fifth, the odd number.

"I know you're probably feeling like complete shit because your parents aren't coming on visiting day," says Summer, the voice of total empathy, "but you know what? At least you have two parents who love you. My parents split up when I was five, and my sister is the only one that they ever loved."

No one says anything.

"What do you mean?" Bunny says, finally, breaking the silence.

"I was sent to live with my grandmother in Wisconsin," Summer says, "and my sister moved to L.A. with my mother. Now she's an actress and she's famous, and beautiful and rich and . . ."

"Thin?" Faith asks, archly.

"That's right," Summer says, gnawing at her cuticle. I noticed the other day that her nails were bitten down to the quick. It looked gross. I stare across at her and she sits without moving. Suddenly she jumps up and runs out of the bunk. Nobody moves for a few seconds, and then simultaneously, all of us spring to our feet and follow her. She's on her knees out behind the bunk, sobbing. Faith kneels down next to her and puts an arm around her shoulders.

"It'll be okay," she says, as if she's trying to reassure a small child. "You can't torture yourself. You're doing the best that you can with your life. We're all here for you."

"I never had any brothers or sisters around me either," Carla says, in a small voice. "And sometimes I hated it, but maybe in some ways it does make you stronger. You can't depend on anyone, so you do things for yourself."

Summer doesn't say anything, she just keeps crying until finally she draws in a deep quivering breath and stops.

"Sorry," she says, trying to pull herself together. "I shouldn't have fallen apart. I usually don't, I . . ."

What do I want to say? "I really don't care. How can I when you're so mean and heartless to everyone else?" What I do say: "You don't have to apologize. We all have buried feelings." We walk her back and I motion for Faith to meet me in the bathroom.

"Do you think we should tell someone about the throwing up?" Whether or not I like her, she does have a medical issue.

"I don't know—I don't want to get her thrown out or anything," Faith says. "Maybe we should wait and see how bad it is."

Does the camp already know? I doubt it would be the first time that one of their campers was bulimic. Or should we just leave it to them to find out? We go back inside to bed. Two out of five of us have ended up in tears so far. Who will be next?

Newspapers, even camp newspapers, are like hospitals—they never close. So two days later, I'm sitting back to back with Jesse again, pretending that nothing happened.

We talk about the articles that we've put into the next issue, including a goof of a questionnaire:

Your Feelings About Your Fat.

The headline is followed by a boldface warning:

CAUTION: Before undertaking this or any other quiz, be sure to check with your doctor or shrink to make sure that you can handle the naked truth.

After all the bogus questions about how you view yourself and your ass, we broke the categories down into four types:

1. Fat and Fun
2. Fat and Fantastic
3. Fat and Just Gross
4. Fat and a Fucking Failure

"Think it'll fly?" Jesse asks, eyebrows raised, after we hand in the copy.

"If they don't read it."

"The dingbat office manager's too busy doing her crosswords to read the camp rag," he says.

"That's good," I say, "because I wrote another one that I want to put on the opposite page." I hand it to him.

WHAT SHAPE IS YOUR BUTT?

I got the idea after reading a quiz about determining the shape of your face so that you could pick the most flattering eyeglass frames. Except *this* quiz had questions like:

- When you look in a rearview mirror, is your ass round like a pumpkin?
- Square like a box?
- Ovoid like a dinosaur egg?
- Completely shapeless, like a rump roast? Here's how to tell:

Jesse reads it and doubles over, laughing so hard he looks like he's in pain. "This definitely kicks ass," he says, gasping for air. I pull it back from him and stick it in a folder that we leave for the secretary, marked NEWSPAPER COPY. I get up, ready to go to my next activity, nutrition class, when he turns to me.

"Your parents coming up for visiting day?"

I look away and then back at him. "Sore subject," I say, with a tight smile. "My mom has to go out to the West Coast. What about your dad?"

He snickers and shakes his head.

"Wanna hang out together?"

"Sure," he says. "I'd rather be with you anyway."

"I'd rather be with you too," I say, realizing that I really mean it. I know I'm blushing, but I don't care. He puts his arms around me and gently leans down and kisses the side of my neck. It's a light kiss, and maybe it doesn't mean much, but I can feel the buzz all the way down to my toes. So just maybe it won't turn out to be that terrible a thing that my parents won't be coming up.

FOURTEEN

o you know how when things are going so ecstatically well that you realize at some point that you're in for a crash landing? Things can't possibly stay at that exalted level of happiness, no matter what. Sooo, the next letter I get from Evie sounds as though she has skydived down from her fantasy perch in heaven with Seth and has rubbed her face into the mud. Even before reading it, it hits me that either she has done it with him or that he wanted her to and broke up with her because she didn't.

Dear Cam: Four more weeks of camp and I can't imagine how I can possibly get through the rest of it now.

THINGS JUST TOTALLY SUCK HERE. I just can't stomach this place.

Seth IS NOT the guy I thought he was. *Let's leave it at that for now. Maybe I was so crazy about him that I was blind to how badly he wanted me to sleep with him and that he obviously didn't care how I felt about it, but believe me when I tell you that you should not trust people you've just met. What happens, at least I think, is that you put all your own wishes and feelings about who they are onto that person and you become blind to who they really are. So now, bottom line, when I'm not playing tennis, I'm on my own, mostly in the camp library. Seth immediately hooked up with another girl in my bunk—if you can imagine—who, first, is totally obnoxious and, second, is a complete slut. The only reason that she's seeing him is because she knows that it makes me foam at the mouth to see them together.*

More than anything, I wish that you were here so that we could talk about this because, Cam, you're the only one in the whole world who I totally trust and believe in. Thank God you picked another camp, not this one.

Write soon,
Love, Evie

I don't care how terrible this sounds, I will say it. Now that Evie's happiness bubble has burst, I feel as though at last she's back to being my best friend, someone I can relate to again. It's not that I want her to be unhappy, just the opposite; it's only that when she was so out of touch with reality she turned into a caricature of herself, someone who belonged on a spoof of a TV show. I felt as though I didn't know her anymore. It was like she had become this shallow, characterless version of herself who was playing the role of "the totally ecstatic girlfriend." I immediately pick up my pen and start writing back to her. Now I have a lot to say:

Dear Evie: I completely understand. And you know what? I think that it just wasn't meant to be. He is clearly not the one. You should just be happy that it's over so you can move on. Honestly, I began to wonder about you and Seth, because everything started up so fast and was so hot and heavy right after you got to camp. Not that I'm a big expert on love or anything, but I mean, things just can't heat up that fast! How could you fall so in love with someone you didn't even have a chance to get to know?

And me? Well, my parents aren't coming on visiting day because my mom has to go to L.A. to see some film director who's buying her book to turn it into a movie. Should I be happy about that? I'm not—I'm royally pissed, because everyone else's parents (except Jesse's) will be here. But now I'm thinking that it's okay, because the two of us have decided to hang out together and I think he really likes me and I'm getting into being with him, because like me, he's more of an outsider than an insider.

More soon. Keep the faith.

Love,

Cam

Whenever a camp opens its doors to parents and visitors, the staff knock themselves out preparing an outrageous buffet and what have you so that the parents believe their kids are eating that way all through the summer. What a joke! As if we EVER saw California rolls, dragon rolls, or exotic boats of sashimi served on glossy red plates with lacquered chopsticks. Or platters of king crab legs. Or pyramids of cold shrimp, except for one time when the refrigerator broke down and they had to go to the fish market in town and buy something ready-made to serve us.

So the parents ooh and aaah over the food and the way the table is set with these rare tropical fresh flowers that look as though they were flown in from Hawaii. It wouldn't have surprised me if Mel walked in wearing a black silk robe, bowing respectfully.

It's pretty much a free-for-all for campers who stay at camp, because most don't. They immediately jump ship and literally go to town with their parents to eat real food (because nobody ever got fat on one meal) as it has been four weeks since camp started and we gave up the freedom to choose.

Jesse and I make circles around the buffet table, snaring shrimp and crab legs. Then we hike to a grassy area over a hill, behind the ball field.

"I come here sometimes when there's a free period," he says. He points into the distance. "There's a cool view back there." He grabs my hand to take me. "I feel like I'm the only one in the world when I'm here," he says, smiling wistfully. "It's my private kingdom."

I look around at the tall fir trees and the view down over jagged boulders to a valley below us and a nearby pond. Aside from one or two houses tucked into the mountains in the distance, it's like our private paradise. I hate camping out—still, I try to imagine what it would be like to sleep out under the stars with Jesse. We sit on a grassy spot and he swings his guitar around in front of him and is about to play it.

"Teach me how to play." He puts the strap around my neck instead, and takes the fingers of my left hand and positions them in different awkward ways, trying to show me the chords. I press hard against the strings and then try strumming.

"I guess it takes practice."

"Years," he says. "But the more you play, the more you get into it." I keep trying to hold my left hand the way he showed me, but eventually the strings leave purple ridges on my fingertips and it feels as though they're about to bleed.

"It must be like exercise—you have to build up tolerance." I slip the strap off my neck and pass the guitar back to Jesse. But instead of playing, he places it next to him on the ground and stretches out on his back, staring up at the sky. He closes his eyes and I study his face. A stubbly chin. Does he shave? It doesn't look like he really has to, though. Dark eyelashes, a straight nose, and a bottom lip with a small white scar in the corner.

"Do you wish you were back home?" I ask.

"Right now?"

"You know what I mean."

"No, there's no one to go home to anyway, except the housekeeper."

"What about your mom?"

He shakes his head. "She split one day to go to California with someone." He looks at me and then closes his eyes again, as though he's protecting his privacy.

"She just walked out?"

"Yep."

"Do you ever see her?"

"She wanted to be single," he says, matter-of-factly. "No kids, no husband. Thought family life was a dead-end." He shrugs. "I don't know where she is."

"How old were you?"

"Ten," he says, exhaling loudly. "That's when I gained the weight. Fifty pounds."

I lay down next to him and put my head on his chest. He puts an arm around me.

"I hate her," I say.

"I hated her too, every day for a long time. Now I don't give a shit anymore."

"Yes you do," I whisper. He doesn't say anything, and we lay together like two people apart from the rest of the world. His T-shirt is soft against my cheek and I feel protected, cuddled up against him with his arm around me. I know that he's as aware of me against him as I am of him, as though there are these chemical messages going back and forth between us. As if in response to what I'm thinking, he turns to his side to face me and tilts his head down to kiss me. It's a real kiss now, not like the one before. His lips are warm and soft and he tastes like the peppermint candies that were on the lunch table. I move closer to him and we lay like that, as if we've melded into one person, until the next thing I realize is that I was asleep. I look at my watch.

"Jesse, we have to get back," I say, shaking him.

"What time is it?" he asks, opening his eyes.

"Four—visiting time is over."

We're up and walking back toward camp with our arms around each other's waist. "I wish I didn't have to go back to my bunk," I say.

"Everybody else went into town today and out to eat. Why don't we go, tonight?"

"How?"

"Let's just go. Hitch, walk, whatever," he says, obviously excited by the idea. "They won't miss us, and we'll get a break from this place."

"It could get us thrown out," I say, biting my lip. "I don't know."

"There's a restaurant in town called the Copper Lantern," he says, ignoring that. "I'll buy you dinner. We can be back before the lights go out." He looks at me, expectantly. "C'mon, Cam, it'll be fun."

Everything with me is always so premeditated. I rarely

act on impulse. Even Evie has said that. She's always the one who tries to egg me on to do things. I want to be with Jesse, he wants to take me out to dinner. Why am I hesitating?

"Let's do it," I say. "Where should we meet?"

"Here, at seven. Go to the evening activity so they see your face, and make sure that your counselor notices you're there. Then back off and slowly drift away. They'll never notice. I'll meet you here."

I lean toward him and kiss his cheek. "Till later."

I race back toward my bunk, the excitement rising in me. How completely cool to just sneak off with Jesse to go out to dinner. We'll eat what we want—large portions, small, whatever, no caloric limits, no foods that have gone from the food scale onto the plate. We'll have a bread basket on the table with tiny gold rectangular packets of real butter. Mashed potatoes with cream, steak rimmed with charred fat, Salads with blue cheese dressing, dessert, and best of all, we'll be together. A real date—my first, although I'd never admit it, not counting the time that Evie's cousin asked me if he could come with me to the movies and then paid for my pizza. I look at my watch and count the hours. I'm excited, nervous, anxious, checking my watch every few minutes, willing it to go faster.

FIFTEEN

The entertainment for tonight is a magic show. Ironic. Hopefully no one will see me and Jesse fade away to pig out. And if his fake ID works, we'll even have Buds instead of Diet Cokes.

The magician is good. I'm almost sorry that I'll miss the last part of his show. He throws knives into the back of his female helpmate, makes words disappear on the pages of books, and does the usual cool stuff like pulling a rabbit out of his top hat. About an hour into it I go to the bathroom. On the way back, I walk past Karen to make sure that she sees me get into my seat.

The second time I get up is during applause at the end of a trick. Just as they're about to break for intermission,

I ease back further and further, finally slipping out of the theater. Outside, I look around. I don't see anyone, so I break into a run.

The air is cool now and there's a good breeze. I sprint across the fields. It's clear that I'm in better shape now than when I got here, four weeks ago. I'm not gasping for air, and running is actually comfortable. If I had company, I could go for miles. After a few minutes, I reach the spot in the hills where Jesse and I agreed to meet, only he's not there. It's quiet except for the steady whine of insects buzzing. Is this totally crazy? I'm out here in the dark, alone, no one knows I'm here, not even Faith. If my parents *ever* knew . . . The sharp sound of a cracking branch makes me dash behind the nearest tree. My heart starts to pound. If Jesse doesn't show up in the next thirty seconds, I'm going to run back, because I'm getting totally freaked. Then the sound of the cracking branch is followed by a hiss, and then his laugh.

"Over here, babe," he says. "I just wanted to see how long it took you to figure out that it was me." I run to him, overwhelmed with relief and grinning like an idiot. He drapes his arm around my shoulder. "Ready to escape from Alcatraz?"

We make our way out of the front gate and start walking along the side of the narrow two-lane country road that leads to town. It's less than five miles, not too bad even if we get stuck walking both ways. But we're so anxious to get into town to have dinner that we decide to hitch.

"Stand on the road and put your thumb out," Jesse says, as if he's done this before. "Girls get picked up a lot faster than guys. When a car stops, I'll run out and get in with you."

I stand waiting along the side of the narrow paved road while Jessie ducks down beneath a clump of trees, out of sight. As soon as I see the headlights of a car, I hold out my thumb. But the car passes and so does the next one, neither of them even slowing down. My guess is that on a dark country road, no one welcomes the sight of a hitchhiker.

"What if the police stop?" I yell out to Jesse. "We would be so screwed."

"They're sitting back in the station," he says, "they're not out looking for hitchhikers." A truck comes down the road and slows, but then the driver floors the gas and speeds away. "Thanks," I call out after him.

"I think we may end up walking; it doesn't look like anybody's game."

"Let's give it another few minutes," Jesse says. "I'd rather not drag my sorry ass into town, since we'll be back doing enough exercise tomorrow."

I turn to look back at Jesse. It hasn't escaped me that he's lost weight. He looks leaner now than when I first met him, and his arms are firmer and more sculpted. The diet and weight lifting were paying off. I don't say anything, because I can't think of a way without it sounding like I'm lusting after him.

I was in way better shape too. Did he notice that? The last time we were weighed in, the scale showed I'd lost just a little over ten pounds—not as much as I had hoped, but from the way that my clothes fit, it made a major difference. I was down at least one size. The exercise was doing its part too, because the measuring tape showed that my thighs and upper arms had gotten smaller. Evie was the only one who knew that ever since I had met Jesse, I was more motivated than ever.

I'm still standing there, about ready to give up, when a convertible drives up with the top down. The driver slows as if he's checking out who's hitching and then comes to a stop. He's not too much older than we are.

"Where you headed?"

"To town, to the Copper Lantern." He motions for me to get in, and a moment later Jesse springs out of the bushes and is at my side. We squeeze into the front seat, and as we pull onto the road, the driver tells us that he's an actor and he's in the area working in the summer theater.

"Not really such a hot idea to hitch," he says, shaking his head. "You're lucky I stopped."

"You get mostly locals on these roads," Jesse says, brushing it aside. The driver doesn't say anything, and minutes later he stops in front of the restaurant.

"Thanks, man," Jesse says. I wave.

"Where you coming from?" he asks, almost as an afterthought.

"Camp Calliope."

"That explains it," he says, with a laugh. I snicker as he pulls away and Jesse turns to me. "Ready to feast?"

I reach for his hand, so psyched.

As I study the menu, I imagine how prison camp inmates must feel after being deprived of decent food, and how they must fantasize about what they need and want. I'm transfixed by a giant blackboard listing grilled hanger steak, filet mignon, 12-ounce hamburgers, veal chops, meatloaf, grilled sausage and peppers, and shrimp scampi, and I want to cry out in anticipation.

After eyeing the entrées, I scan the "sides": Garlic

mashed potatoes, bourbon whipped sweet potatoes, cottage fries, wild rice, Caesar salad, and house salad with blue cheese dressing. We start with garlic bread and baked clams, and for the main course, hanger steak, mashed potatoes, and salad.

"What do you guys want to drink?"

Jesse looks up at the waiter, not at me. "A Heineken," he says casually.

"Can I see your ID?"

He pulls a card out of his wallet and holds it up. In the semidark it must look authentic, because the waiter nods and turns to me.

"Iced tea."

He turns and I grin at Jesse. I know that he has just turned sixteen. "Where did you get it?"

"The East Village."

I had heard that it was easy to get fake IDs in Greenwich Village.

"For ten bucks, you can buy a new identity," he says.

We wait as other tables around us get their orders, teased by the scent of grilled meat as platters are carried over our heads to other tables. When the garlic bread and clams are put between us, Jesse tears off a piece of bread and offers it to me. I take a bite and tear off a piece for him. We share the clams with their buttery golden breadcrumb topping, and when the plate is empty, I look over at him, suddenly overcome with anxiety.

"What if we get kicked out of camp?"

"Why should we?"

"If they find out."

He shakes his head. "They won't, but if they do, here's the story—we were under psychological strain. Our parents didn't come to visit us, everybody else was taken out to dinner, it was depressing for us, blah blah blah." He smiles. "They'll end up feeling sorry for us, if they find out, but they won't."

"Do you feel sorry for us—for yourself?"

He shrugs. "No, yeah, I don't know." He takes a sip of beer. "Whatever."

"Do you ever really talk to your father, try to get through to him?"

"Not anymore."

"Why?"

"Because he doesn't love me," he says, flatly.

"Are you sure?"

"He loves his team," he says, a flash of anger in his eye. "He gives them everything that he has. When he comes home again he's wiped out. The only one he wants to see is his massage therapist." He takes another sip of beer and then stares off into the distance. "I'm a reminder of a part of his life that he screwed up, and my dad doesn't like to screw up. So he's decided to become blind to that."

Before I can answer, the steaks come and we fixate on the food.

"Omigod," I say, slicing off one piece of steak and then another. It's charred on the outside and pink inside, just the way I love it. I reach across the table and slide his beer over to me.

"Oh, man," he keeps saying, like a mantra, while he shakes his head.

I take one sip, then another. "I like it," I say, with a laugh.

He pulls it back. "I figured that you would." We finish the bottle and he orders another one. We're so busy filling our stomachs that we don't talk much. Jesse may be relaxed, but I can't help keeping my eye on the door. What if some of the counselors walk in, or worse still, Mel? It's a small town, and there aren't too many places to go outside of camp other than this place, the Dairy Queen, or the two fast-food restaurants. I highly doubt that the staff subsists on camp food all summer.

I can't help thinking about how my parents would react if they got a call about me leaving camp and hitching into town for dinner. And the beer? The worst scenario would be my getting thrown out of camp while they

were in L.A. making the movie deal. They'd visit then, in
a hurry.

The restaurant is filling up with locals who are talking
loudly, laughing, drinking, and smoking, and I get a flash
of me being ten years older, sitting with Jesse as if he were
my husband. Never mind weight loss, we'd both be overweight, middle-aged, paunchy. I try to get that thought
out of my head. It's only one meal. One night. Then we'll
go back to our diets, get back on track.

"What?" Jesse says.

"What what?"

"You looked kinda down suddenly," he says, "what's
wrong?"

"I was imagining us eating this way every night for the
rest of our lives."

He scratches the back of his head and laughs wryly, tilt-
ing his chin up toward an overweight guy who is too big
for the chair he's sitting on. "That would be me."

The waiter comes back and begins clearing away our
empty plates. "You guys have room for dessert?" We exchange glances and of course now that I'm already full,
the guilt factor is starting to kick in.

"One," he says, seeing my face. "We'll share it."

"Chocolate layer cake," I say.

Of course it's enough for four, and it comes with two

forks. We take turns. "Omigod," I keep saying. Jesse just stares at me across the table and laughs.

"This is fun," he says. "I'm glad we did it . . . and I'm glad I met you. I don't know how I could have gotten through the summer without you."

"I'm glad I met you too," I say, smiling back at him. The truth is the last thing I expected was that I'd meet a boy I liked at camp. I would have counted myself lucky just making one girlfriend. I don't know how I get up the nerve, but I look up at him and ask him something that I've been wanting to know. "Have you ever had a girl-friend?"

He shakes his head. "There was one girl in school who I liked for a while, but she didn't know I existed," he says. "It was the weight I guess . . . or maybe she just thought that I was a complete jerk."

"What about you?"

I shake my head.

"Can I be your first boyfriend?" he asks, narrowing his eyes.

I stare down at the table, suddenly overcome. "You are," I say, so low I don't know if he heard me. He reaches across the table and takes my hand.

"Cool," he says, "very cool."

Then, like Cinderella, I look up at the clock and realize that it's ten o'clock, and my panic alarm goes off. "We
have half an hour to get out of here and be in our bunks,"
I say. "I can't believe it's so late."

Without a word, Jesse gets up and goes up to the cash
register to pay the check, and after he goes back to toss a
few bills on the table, we start running toward the highway. It's raining now and we didn't expect that. We're
standing on the edge of the road with our thumbs out,
getting soaked. There are very few cars on the road, and
because it seems pointless to just stand still and wait any
longer, I start to run because there's no way we're going to
make it back in time.

"Jesus," Jesse says, trying to keep up with me. "I'm so
full, I don't think that I can do this."

"I know," I say, breathless, slowing down. "I'm starting
to feel sick myself." We slow to a fast walk, keeping our
eyes on the highway to make sure that we're ready for on
coming cars. One goes by and then another.

"Shit, what are we going to do?" Now I'm definitely
panicking.

"Someone will come along," he says, as though he's trying to convince himself. But no one does, until we hear
the roar of a motor coming up the road and then see the

outline of a truck. It's a large food truck with Texas plates. The driver slows and then comes to an abrupt stop just a few yards down the road from where we're standing. We run up to it and the side window rolls down.

"C'mon, get in," he yells. The passenger door opens out to us, and I take a huge step up with Jesse right behind me.

SIXTEEN

"So we're at the halfway point," Susan says, nodding her head for emphasis, "and I hope that by now it's clear to all of you that what we're trying to accomplish is to encourage you to look and feel better not by dieting or following some strict, short-term regimen that has failure written all over it, but by changing the way you live." She looks around the room.

She's talking about changing the way we live by changing our eating habits, but for me, her words take on a more cosmic meaning. Just ten hours earlier, in the dark of night, I ran off as much for the food as the freedom. It was breakout time. I was sick of eating the measured portions of *their* foods. I wanted to eat what I wanted, and I wanted to be alone with Jesse, away from prison camp.

On some level, maybe I even wanted to get caught to punish my parents. But things didn't turn out the way I expected. On the way home, things spun out of control.

Five pools of yellow light illuminate the rafters, creating shadows like heavenly beacons.

"So I have to come clean," Bunny says. "I'm a candy junkie and I've been buying candy bars from this sleazy thief who works in the kitchen. It's just something that my body needs to have. But this guy is such a total rip-off artist—five dollars for a Mars bar. I'd like to get him fired, but I need my fix and I don't care."

"I can't believe you would do that," Carla says.

"What, eat candy?" Bunny is obviously annoyed. "No, I didn't think you'd understand."

"No, buy it from him," Carla says. "It's like we're food addicts and he's selling the drug that we have to stay away from."

"Welcome to the real world," Summer says.

I sit there, not saying anything, hoping that no one will notice the fact that I'm not taking part, but I'm wrong.

"What do you think, Cam?" Bunny asks. "You've been so quiet lately. What's going on with you?"

"Nothing." Everyone stares. "I'm just bored with every-thing," I throw in because I feel I need to explain.

"So what do you think?" Bunny insists, repeating her original question.

"About?"

"About selling candy."

"I think we should report him and get him fired. He's a cheater, and I hate that. Our parents paid thousands of dollars to send us here. Why should we let him sabotage us?" I didn't intend to sound so angry, but the frustration was welling up in me.

Faith turns to me. "Wow, why the born-again, goody-goody attitude? Are you becoming a preacher for the overweight?"

"We came here to lose weight," I tell her, clicking off my flashlight. "If we're buying candy bars on the side and cheating, what's the point?" I get up and pause for a sec-ond before walking back to my bed. "Life catches up with you . . . when you screw up and compromise yourself, life has a way of throwing you a curve and teaching you a les-son."

SEVENTEEN

So I sound preachy and self-righteous. So what? I had been scared out of my mind, and like shock therapy, it rewired my brain.

At least Jesse was with me and I have him to talk to. We learned something together and I wouldn't be able to keep that to myself. What I know for sure, though, is that our night away won't be the subject of a rap session, but I'm not sure why. Am I ashamed? Embarrassed? Or is it just that it isn't anybody else's business? I had learned a lesson, and the fact that we got out of it, alive and safe, is something that I'll never forget.

*   *   *

After dinner, we left the restaurant and turned back toward the road, ready to hitch. We left later than we should have so we didn't have time to walk. It was dark out, pitch-black, actually. There were no lights along the country road, not even moonlight to help us find the way. The only light came from the sudden beams of headlights as cars snaked past us, without stopping.

What we hadn't counted on was the weather. There were crashes of distant thunder after we left the restaurant, and then minutes later it started to storm. The rain was pouring down in one of those intense storms that build up in the mountains in the late afternoon or evening. Why didn't we think that it might rain, and how that might have complicated things?

The sky was shot with lightning that resembled metallic fireworks. Deep claps of thunder pounded like kettle drums. We were dressed in only jeans and T-shirts. No raincoats. No umbrellas. In seconds our clothes were clinging to us, soaked. We huddled together, ducking down under bushes to make ourselves lower to the ground whenever we saw lightning.

I had eaten too much, I knew that the minute I left the restaurant. Since I had avoided heavy, greasy meals for a month, my stomach wasn't used to the rich food or the large portions, so appealing when they were put down on the table in front of us an hour earlier. Then there was the beer: Just a few sips and it went to my head. I felt shaky, off balance. I didn't expect that—I thought that it took more for you to feel it.

One car went by and then another, but no one stopped. What was the point of standing there with my thumb in the air? I looked back at Jesse unsure, and he just shook his head as if he didn't know what to say.

"Let's keep walking," he said, finally, his arm slung around me. "We can make it in about forty minutes if we hurry." What he didn't have to say was that we'd be late for curfew and that everybody would know it. By morning, it would be common knowledge that the two of us sneaked out. We were both cold and shivering, but we didn't talk about that.

I usually don't take risks like this. I'm the type who does what I'm supposed to. So naturally, the one time I took a chance, it looked like I'd get caught. I was startled out of my thoughts by the roar of a large truck coming around the curve. My arm shot up and I used my thumb to point in the direction of the camp. The truck slowed and then the wheels made a sharp sound as the driver came to a stop along the gravelly edge of the road. I looked up at Jesse and he smiled.

"Bingo," he said.

It came as an enormous relief. Just when we had given up finding a ride. I couldn't wait to get inside where it was warm and dry. We'd be back at camp in minutes, and I was already fantasizing about getting out of my wet clothes and changing into a dry T-shirt and getting into bed under my heavy blanket. In the morning, the whole thing would be a memory and I'd get back to the diet and the business of losing weight.

The metal door on the passenger side of the truck swung open and I ran over to it, lifting my leg up to climb onto the high step. Jesse clambered in after me, and I slid over next to the driver to make room. The vinyl seat was old and torn, and I felt a sharp edge catch against the smooth fabric of my worn jeans. Jesse slammed the heavy door shut, and the driver looked over at us before turning the wheel sharply to get back onto the road.

"Where you two headed?" he asked. That was when my heart started to pound. His breath reeked of alcohol, and as I looked at him I saw that he was squinting his eyes as if he had trouble focusing.

"Just a few miles up on the road," Jesse said. He reached over and squeezed my hand momentarily. I glanced at him and he nodded almost imperceptively.

"So let's get goin'." He stepped on the gas and then turned back and smiled at me. "So how are you doing tonight?" he asked, patting my thigh.

"Okay," I said. I tried to slide closer to Jesse without it looking obvious.

"Don't see too many hitchhikers anymore," he said. He laughed. "Aren't you kids afraid?"

"Of what?" I asked, in a hoarse whisper.

"You never know who you're getting into a car with," he said, softly, staring at me more than the road. I kept my eyes ahead of me, watching the rain flood the windshield and the way the wipers kept automatically trying to wipe it away, again and again, no match for the force of the water. I was wearing a thin white cotton shirt that was clinging to me, and I could feel a puddle of water forming on the seat around me as it dripped off my hair and shirt. I started to shiver, almost uncontrollably.

"Yeah, well, we're together," Jesse said, to remind him that he was there. "Everybody up here hitches."

For some reason the driver seemed to find that funny. "Yeah," he said with a gruff laugh. He leaned forward to turn on the radio, switching it from one station to another, punching at the buttons, looking down more than up at the road, annoyed because he couldn't find what he was looking for. He kept cursing under his breath. "Never a goddamn thing on," he said. "Stupid people callin' in . . ."

"I'll do that so that you concentrate on the road," I said.

He was quiet for a moment and then turned to me. "You think I can't drive?" he hissed. I watched his face change and grow hard. I knew that I had said the wrong thing.

"No, it's just that—"

"You think I can't drive this goddamn truck and turn the radio without some kid helping me?" His voice was getting louder and I felt my heart start to thump wildly. "You're brats," he said, spitting out the word as though it were a curse. "I was trying to help you out, pick you up out of the rain, but you're spoiled little brats." His foot pressed harder on the gas pedal.

"Look, man, if you want to let us out here, that's fine," Jesse said. "We're sorry to trouble you." But the driver didn't seem to hear him. He stared ahead as though he were obsessed with his own thoughts and his own frustrations. We were approaching the gates of the camp, but he kept going.

"WAIT, this is IT, STOP, PLEASE!" I yelled, but he passed the entrance gate and kept driving. I turned to Jesse and he shook his head. About a mile up the road, the driver started to slowly swerve into the lane of oncoming traffic. It was dark, no one else was on the road. Was anyone coming? It was raining so hard there was no way I could tell. Where was he taking us? I looked at him to see how tall and strong he was. There were two of us, and Jesse was taller, bigger. But none of that mattered then, because at that moment, in the distance, I saw a tiny pool of light that was growing larger as it came closer and closer, and then I realized that I was seeing headlights of an approaching car in the opposite lane.

"JESUS, WATCH OUT, YOU'RE GOING TO HIT HIM!" Jesse screamed before I could open my mouth. Instinctively, he pulled his knees against his chest and grabbed me toward him. The driver swerved hard to the right just in time, getting out of the way, but then slammed on his brakes as if at the last moment it dawned on him what was about to happen. But he stopped too abruptly. I looked up in horror when I saw the eyes of a small deer that had stopped on the side of the road ahead of us, frozen with fear. The next thing I heard was the loud thwack.

"Oh, God, NO!" I shrieked as we skidded off the road. I was thrown into Jesse as the truck bumped and veered wildly to the right, finally slamming an embankment before jerking to a stop. Jesse's arm slammed the window, and I saw him wince with pain. We sat there immobile for one second, then another, frozen, listening to the rain pelting the windshield. The driver stared ahead of him, stunned, as if he were dumbstruck. He was so still that it occurred to me for a brief second that he might be dead, but then I saw him shake his head slightly.

Jesse was the first to react. He jerked the door open wide and jumped down, pulling me after him. "You're drunk out of your mind you stupid bastard," he yelled, seething with rage. I jumped down so hard that I landed on my knees, but Jesse pulled me to my feet by the arm. Before I ran, I stopped momentarily and stared at the deer. The poor, sad creature lay on his side, his eyes open now, unblinking, staring at nothing. In a millisecond, his life was snuffed out. Over. Gone, because of a drunk driver, rain, and the unspeakable horrors that can happen in an instant that change your world forever.

Blood was everywhere. "Oh, my God," I said, pulling my hands up to my mouth.

"We have to go," Jesse insisted, dragging me away. We started running as fast as we could, keeping off the road and heading into the bushes. I turned to see if he would come after us, but we didn't stop to find out and kept going until I let go of his hand, leaned over, and threw up. Then I started to shake, uncontrollably, and the tears poured out of me.

"I know," Jesse whispered, holding me. "I'm sorry, Cam. I'm so sorry."

"We were so close to getting killed," I whispered, when I could catch my breath. "I think of that deer . . ."

"It's over," he said, his eyes filling with tears. "It's over."

EIGHTEEN

Their cream-colored Lexus pulls into the half-empty camp lot and they ease into the very first free parking space, next to the handicapped spot. The side window rolls down before the car comes to a stop.

"CAM!" my mom calls out, excitedly, waving. I smile and wave back. I am so psyched to see them, but I don't realize that until they're in front of me. Real. It's been four weeks, but it seems like months. I feel as though I have to meet them again, get to know them all over. They're my parents, but it feels that there's a gap between us that we have to cross to get back to where we were.

I was given the entire day off to be with them, free to wander around, leave for lunch, and follow my schedule or not. Not. No way I'd follow the routine with them sitting on the sidelines watching me sweat. But since they want to stay at camp to get a feeling for what my day is like, I asked for box lunches so we can picnic and then tour the place.

What I didn't tell them before—to avoid the inevitable barrage of questions—was that there would be four of us spending the day together, not three. Since his dad wasn't coming up, Mel said it was okay if Jesse joined me and my parents.

It shouldn't have surprised us that he said yes. At Camp Calliope, in fact, visiting day is viewed as almost a religious experience that every camper is entitled to. That's one view, anyway. The other is that parents are footing the bill, so the camp director practically genuflects in their presence.

Anyway, I know what you're thinking, and the answer to your question is no. Mel never found out about our ill-fated dinner out. The whole night was like a short story that ends up with a twist at the end. What happened was that the bad storm had entirely thrown off the evening schedule. Nobody wanted to go back to their bunks when there was so much lightning, so everyone hung around for almost an extra hour singing camp songs after the magic show was over. When I finally made it back to the bunk, soaking wet, everyone else was just getting back too, and I think it never occurred to Karen that I wasn't with them. There were raised eyebrows and a few whispered remarks about where I was, but nobody had a clue that we were off the camp grounds.

It's not like there weren't other unexplained absences. Carla was out late one night with Trevor and we covered for her. And Bunny, well it wasn't clear where she was, although Faith and I suspected that it had something to do with chasing Rick. So no one said anything, even Summer, the queen bitch, and I got a free ticket out of jail.

When you haven't seen your parents for a while—and when they haven't seen you—you notice things that you probably wouldn't if you had been with them without interruption. My mom looks tan and very fit. She's wearing designer jeans, a fitted white Lacoste shirt, and awesome Pumas.

"Cool," I say, pointing to them. Unfortunately I can't hope to inherit them, because she wears one size smaller than I do. My dad looks as though his slight paunch is flatter, and for a father, he looks hip in khaki cargo pants and a black T-shirt. Maybe my parents look better than I remember because they've been on vacation—from me.

My mom beams when she sees me, and I go running

into her arms. My dad gets the next hug. I can tell that they're relieved I'm not still carrying a grudge about their missing visiting day. I wouldn't bring it up and I knew they wouldn't revisit it.

"You look just fabulous," my mom pronounces, as her eyes scan me from head to toe. "And makeup," she says, obviously impressed that I have discovered its powers. My father just bobs his head in agreement, speechless for the first time in as long as I can remember.

I did lose more weight than I expected, but it came at a price. In addition to the dieting and exercise, after the night out with Jesse I was so shaken by what we went through and what could have happened that I kept throwing up, eventually losing my appetite for days— which has never happened to me before. The blank stare of that pathetic deer kept haunting my thoughts. The *bad* news was that I felt completely sick and couldn't shake it. The *good* news was that I actually dropped another three pounds. Karen was convinced that it was viral and made me go to the infirmary.

"Probably just a stomach bug," the camp doctor said, because he had no clue, and anyway, I always assume that camp doctors are like low on the totem pole or otherwise why would they be camp doctors? "Do you want me to call your parents?" he asked.

"Oh, no, don't," I said, the words tumbling out of my mouth in a rush. "It would just worry them. I'm fine, really." He didn't call, and I avoided what would have been a long interrogation. He prescribed bed rest and fluids, which was just fine with me.

But now, here I am, basking in the praise from them that I thought I'd be immune to by now. So much for independence and my stalwart sense of self. I wasn't sure how they'd react when they saw me. It was obvious that they saw more progress than I did.

"Well, it hasn't been easy," I say, when they ask how well I'm holding up. "In general, the food here is totally gross." I look at Jesse for confirmation and he nods in agreement. It's only then that I think they focus on him and realize that he's going to hang out with us.

"This is my friend, Jesse," I say, when it hits me that they don't know who he is and that I should have introduced him. "He's going to hang out with us, if that's okay."

"Of course," my mom says, almost a little too heartily.

"His dad couldn't make it up here on visiting day either," I say, "so I asked if he could join us."

"Absolutely," my dad says, echoing my mom.

"I'll show you around," I say, awkwardly, leading them on what turns out to be about a two-mile tour of every part of the place, from the gym to the theater.

"We walk up and down these hills about a hundred times a day," I say, as we make our way back down to the mess hall.

"Well, it's a pretty walk," my mom says, trying as usual to be upbeat. Although we wanted to visit the camp before we booked it, we never found a weekend when everybody was free, so we watched a fast-moving video instead—complete with thrilling upbeat disco music—and depended on references from kids who had been here before. It only occurs to me now that although some of the counselors are the same, the campers aren't. If those kids had such a rewarding, successful summer, why didn't they come back?

"You should be thrilled that you're away from the city heat and the concrete," my mom says. "It's oppressive." She looks up at the trees. "There's something about being in the country with all the greenery, the heat's just much more bearable."

"How's the summer going for you, Jesse?" my dad asks, turning to him. *God, please don't start one of those stupid man-to-man conversations with him. Don't ask him dumb jock questions about sports or his favorite teams, or I will completely die. And worst of all, don't ask him about his weight.*

"Tolerable," Jesse says with a half-smile.

My father smiles and pats him on the back. I sense that he realizes not to push. At the mess hall we pick up the box lunches that they have ready for us, and we find a place to sit out by the lake. We unwrap the sandwiches and find smoked salmon salad with dill, and tuna salad with dill and chopped olives. There's fresh fruit salad for dessert and lemon wafers, with iced tea and bottled water to drink.

"Nice," my mother says, taking her first bite.

I look over at Jesse. "Comrade, when was the last time you had a smoked salmon salad sandwich?" I ask, narrowing my eyes questioningly

"Hmmm, what year is this?"

"We do not get sandwiches like these when parents aren't around," I say, drily, shaking my head. "This is such a total farce."

"So you'll appreciate your home more than ever when you come back," my mom says brightly. About what I expected.

As we're finishing lunch, Faith, Carla, Bunny, and Summer walk past us on their way to water aerobics. "Wanna workout with us?" Summer calls out, sweetly. Someone who didn't know her would naturally assume that she is kind and friendly and that her invitation is genuine.

"No," I say, matching my tone to hers. "Do an extra set for me, okay?"

Jesse laughs, and my parents just look at me as if they know they're missing something.

We talk about the camp activities, the bunks, the heat, and everything in the universe that falls into the category of trivial, because that's what you do when your parents visit to cover up the fact that the time together feels forced and awkward and all you're thinking about is the time ticking away and the moment when they have to head back to their car and drive home without you and how awkward and terrible it will be.

"So what does your dad do?" my dad slips in, turning to Jesse. Is that a male thing? Men have to know what other men, or at least their fathers, do to assess how much money they make and to see if they measure up.

He pumps gas, I'm tempted to say, to see how that goes over.

"He's a basketball coach," Jesse says, prepared to leave it at that.

"Really?" My dad's assuming that he works for some hick high school in suburban New Jersey or something. "How old are the kids?"

"Actually, they're professional athletes," Jesse says, with a hint of a smile. "The New York Rockets."

That lands with the predictable ten on the Richter scale. My dad looks up as if Jesse said his dad was Lance Armstrong.

"Really?" I can't tell if he's truly bowled over or whether he wants to sound that way to boost Jesse's ego. "You must be proud as hell," he says, convincing me that he really is wowed.

Jesse shrugs, leaving it at that, and he and I exchange brief glances. My mom, who's good at what she does because she has an eye for picking up on subtleties in tone, body language, and what have you, immediately seizes on the fact that there's more to the story. I see that half-quizzical look register in her eyes.

"It must be hard, since he's on the road a lot," she says, attempting to smooth over what she assumes is bumpy territory as well as draw him out. But Jesse isn't biting. He makes some vague expression of agreement and looks off. He doesn't whine, I know that about him already.

I can see that my dad is ready to launch into one of his man-to-man discussions—maybe about basketball, or the hottest players, or even who is ahead for the season, blah, blah, blah, when my mother shoots him one of her cau-

tionary looks. The trial lawyer picks up on it immediately.
Anyway, he and my mother communicate the way people
who have spent decades together do, to the point of finishing each other's sentences.

"So," my mother starts in another direction, looking
back at me. "Tell me about your bunk mates."

I tell her about Faith and her animals and the way
everyone looks up to her because she's the most together
girl in the whole bunk. They laugh when I say, "Mah
Gawd, Cam," imitating her accent. Then I explain,
offhandedly, about Bunny and her candy bar connection,
Carla's depression, and Summer's bulimia. Now it's my
mother who says, "My God," and means it. She's obviously surprised that our little village has so many issues.
It really bothers me that they are so totally naive.

"There are a lot of reasons why people become fat," I
say, indignantly. "Not everyone starts out that way and
grows up with extra fat cells." Both of my parents look at
me, surprised. Are they so wrapped up in their own
worlds that they don't realize the complex sorority that
I'm an unwilling part of? I look over at Jesse, and I know
from that moment that this is something that he and I,
and everyone else who is a teenager and overweight, will
have to deal with on our own for the rest of our lives. It
isn't a thing you can blame on your parents, or someone

else, or a sheer lack of willpower, or any of the other meaningless explanations that try to simplify what isn't.

I don't want to depend on their approval. And it doesn't matter if they disapprove: It is my life, and how I end up looking and weighing and living is up to me.

Jesse knows that too—even better than I do, I think. If he stays heavy or decides to keep on losing, the decision is his. What his father thinks is irrelevant. He doesn't want to be a basketball player, and it doesn't matter if he measures up. It's his life, not his father's, and he has to be comfortable in his own skin.

When Karen comes over to tell us that visiting hours are over, it comes as a relief. I wasn't looking forward to them leaving, but they have to and I want to get it over with.

"We'll miss you," my dad says, giving me a hard hug. "This was great."

"I'll miss you too," I mumble, for lack of anything else to say.

"Keep writing," my mom says. "We look for your letters every day and if we don't get one, we're disappointed."

"Sometimes the mail's screwed up," I say, attempting to explain away what's obvious.

"It was nice meeting you, Jesse," my dad says, patting

him on the shoulder like an old friend. "You too," Jesse says. "Cam's lucky to have you."

I turn and look at Jesse. I didn't expect him to say anything like that. Does he envy me, having a real family? Does it make him realize how little home life he has?

"I hope we see you in the city," my mom adds, touching his arm. "We'd love to have you come over for dinner."

"Thanks," Jesse says. I know he means it.

NINETEEN

You can imagine the way my heart starts slamming against my chest when Karen tells me that Mel wants to see me—"immediately."

How did he find out about me and Jesse? Who could have told him? Was it someone who came into the restaurant? I didn't see anyone, but it was possible that one or two of the counselors came in for a drink and spotted us. Over and over again that stupid phrase "murder outs" keeps streaming through my brain.

If only I could reach Jesse to find out ahead of time what he knows. The damn cell phones don't work up here, and even if they did, he's not walking around with his on and neither is anyone else. The next time I'm supposed to see him is two days later in the newspaper office.

I try for the calm look. "Oh," I say to Karen, acting perplexed. "What's it about?"

"He didn't say," Karen said. "Just said he wanted to see you right now." I can't read anything in her expression, so I assume that she doesn't know whatever it is that Mel does.

I walk across the camp toward the office. *I hope that I don't get kicked out. I hope that he didn't find out what happened. My parents will be so pissed, especially when they were just here and everything seemed so perfect to them. But what's worse, what really scares me, is getting kicked out and not being up here with Jesse.*

When I get to the office, I open the door and surprise, surprise, come face to face with—yes, Jesse. We look at each other expectantly.

"Mel asked to see me," I say in a clipped tone, as though I'm talking in secret code.

"Me too," he says, cocking his head to the side, casually.

"I wonder what it could be about?" I say for the benefit of the secretary.

"Don't know," he says, suddenly studying his sneakers.

Mel calls us in together—at least we're not being interrogated separately to see if our stories match—and in an instant I know. There, on his desk, is the last issue of the newspaper, and I want to burst out laughing. I was so caught up in thinking about our night away that I had totally forgotten about it. It comes as a huge relief that we're about to get our asses fried for something so laughably benign.

And just as an aside, Faith and Summer and everyone in our bunk thought that the quizzes were completely hysterical.

"Oh, mah Gawd," Faith whooped, when she read it. "You are such a humorous bitch."

"Way to go," Summer said. "Just goof on this whole stupid place."

But Mel doesn't quite see it that way. He stares at me and Jesse for a full minute, sizing us up, before exhaling as though it was an extraordinarily hard thing to blow out CO_2.

"Cam, Jesse"—another labored blow out—"I know what your intentions were. I know that you're good kids and that you didn't want to hurt anyone, but . . . but . . ." he says, rubbing his hand up the side of his face, momentarily reaching for the appropriate words for our solemn get-together. "The reason that we're all here is that being overweight is far from a laughing matter." He lets that sink in and goes on to some head shaking. "It's summer, you're kids, and we want to have fun here, but the real reason we're here is a serious one, and to make fun of a serious problem is to potentially hurt someone."

"Sorry," I mumble. Jesse says the same thing, like a distant echo.

"Obviously I can't have anything else like this run in the paper again, and I blame myself as much as anyone, since it's my camp and it was my duty to read the paper before it went to the printer."

I shift from one leg to the other.

"I was hoping that I could give you the independence to do this on your own. I assumed that you'd uphold the standards that the camp has always prided itself on . . . but obviously the system broke down. It didn't work the way I had hoped." He sits at his desk, drumming his pencil against the edge of it.

"It was my fault," Jesse says. "If there's any punishment due, I'm the one who deserves it." I turn and look at him, surprised. Why was he trying to take all the blame?

"It was just as much my fault," I say, "so I—"

"Stop, Cam," Jesse says, and I'm guessing that he's thinking that he has a lot less to lose, since his dad won't care one way or the other if he gets in trouble.

Mel looks at Jesse and then at me and shakes his head, not understanding. "I don't know which of you started it, but it doesn't matter," he says, trying to end the back-and-forth. "The thing that I want to make sure is that this doesn't happen again. The point of a newspaper is to report and inform. It's not put out to make cheap jokes."

We stand there trying to act solemn and repentant, as if we're absorbing the full weight of his words. I want to burst out laughing, both in amusement and relief, so I keep my eyes down, at the floor. Eventually he dismisses us with a warning and a lot more head shaking.

We file out of the office silently, and then when we get out the door we exchange glances and smile.

"Terrible," Jesse says, imitating Mel. "This is a serious problem."

"I should fry your ass, Jesse McKinley," I say, talking in the same tone.

"Just you try it," he says, slapping me on the behind and running off before I can hit him back. I run to catch him, and he turns suddenly, coming at me, tackling me, and throwing me to the ground.

"Pick on someone your own size, Phillips," he says, holding my hands out and pinning them under his. I look up at him and he leans his head down, pressing his lips against mine.

TWENTY

As soon as the bunk's screen door slams, I get this sick feeling in my gut. Something is terribly wrong. Carla is alone, lying on her bed with her head dangling down over the side.

"Carla!" I shriek. "Are you all right? CARLA!" I run over to the bed and climb the ladder. She doesn't answer, and I totally panic.

"CARLA!" I call out her name one more time before starting to bolt to the infirmary for the nurse. *Is she dead?*

"What?" she answers finally, in a soft voice, lifting her head.

"What's wrong with you? Sit up, don't hang your head

over like that. You scared the hell out of me," I say, filled
with relief.

Slowly she sits up. She has a vacant look in her eyes. "What
did you take?" I ask. "Did you overdose on something?"

"No," she says. "I just stopped taking the pills . . .
they . . . they weren't working."

"Stay there," I tell her. "Don't move."

Did *not taking* medicine do that? I never heard of anything like that. Was it worse *not* to take it than to take it?
I run to the infirmary and get the nurse, and on the way
see Karen and tell her about Carla. They call the doctor
and then run back to the bunk with me. The nurse takes
Carla's pulse and listens to her heart, then looks into her
eyes with a flashlight. She gets Carla up and walks her to
the infirmary. I go with them and wait for the doctor to
get there. Karen comes in and sits with Carla.

"Go back to the bunk," Karen says. "We'll let you know
what's up a little later."

"Are you sure? Maybe she wants someone from the
bunk to stay with her."

"Go ahead," Karen insists. "We'll let you know what we
hear as soon as we can."

By the time I get back, the entire camp knows about
Carla, because camp news travels faster than the speed of
light.

"What happened?" Summer asks. "Did she OD on something?"

"How is she?" Faith says, at the same time.

"She stopped taking her medicine, she told me. I guess she had some kind of reaction. The nurse says she thinks she'll be okay, but—" I shake my head. "The doctor's coming, and I guess they'll call her parents."

"She's thin, she's gorgeous, what the hell is *she* so depressed about?" Summer asks, shaking her head. "It's always the *perfect* ones who are so screwed up."

"You're *blaming* her for being depressed?" I want to slap her.

"It's chemical," Bunny says, trying to explain what should be obvious. "It's not her fault. It's like our craving for food . . . it doesn't have to make sense."

"I wonder if they'll send her home," Faith says, as if she's thinking aloud.

"That'll really make her depressed," I say. "I know she's got problems, but I think that she likes it here. If they force her to leave, she'll really feel like she failed."

"Let's go talk to the doctor," Faith says, standing up. "We know her better than they do."

Carla's parents come up to the camp that evening and spend the night at the nearby medical center where they've taken Carla to watch her and make sure that she's really okay. A psychiatrist is called in and so is a pharmacist. Karen comes back to our bunk later and tells us that what happened is that Carla stopped her medication too abruptly, without tapering it off slowly, and she experienced what amounted to severe withdrawal symptoms. They called her doctor in New York, and after a long conference with him and the camp, they decided that it would be better to let her stay at camp. They were putting her on new medications that the nurse would keep. Every morning Carla will have to go there and take it in front of the nurse. If she doesn't, they'll send her home. Meanwhile, they're keeping her at the med center for another full day just to watch her and make sure that she's really okay.

It feels empty in the bunk without her. It isn't our fault, but somehow without her the circle is broken and we can't help but feel that we let her down.

"Maybe we should have watched out more for her," Bunny says. It's dark in the bunk and we're all in our beds.

"How could we have known?" I say. "We all get depressed sometimes, and I don't think she acted so different from any of us—except for the crying."

"My brother was depressed once," Faith says. "We didn't realize until he tried to kill himself, how bad it was."

"Oh God," I whisper. "Is he okay now?"

"It went on for a few months, right after his best friend died in a car accident. He started seeing a shrink and taking medicine, and then he seemed to pull himself out of it." No one says anything. As almost an afterthought, she says, "that's when I gained the weight."

"We've all got secrets," Summer says.

Nobody asks what hers are. I think we're afraid to know.

TWENTY-ONE

As usual, I'm sitting in the first row of nutrition class. It's just a thing with me. I once heard that people who go to the back row of a class are beaming out a message to the teacher that they want to hide. I also heard that if you sit in the first row you do better. I guess it has to do with being forced to pay attention because you don't have anybody's back to study.

Anyway, somewhere along the line I decided that maybe I couldn't do much about my weight, but I could do something about my grades. I also read a book about a girl who was fat and ended up saving the ass of the star football player by helping him pass the exam he needed to ace to stay on the team. After that he never made fun of her again: The only people he made fun of were the ones who made fun of her. That stayed with me, so ever since, I sit in the first row, ready to raise my hand so that they don't have to call on me to see if I'm awake.

Now Susan's talking about keeping food diaries, one of the most boring and ineffective things that you can do to lose weight, as I see it. I've kept lots of those, staying honest at first. But then you get to the point where you feel it doesn't pay to record that tiny sample cube of cheddar cheese in the supermarket, or the one or two mouthfuls of casserole that you scooped out of the pot just after your mother took it out of the oven. And then, fuck it, you just didn't write down anything at all about that dessert called the Great Wall of Chocolate, because the number of calories in it was probably greater than the total number of people in all of China and it would just blow your total effort. So you stop caring and resent that your life is reduced to clinical entries in a food journal. But I don't go into all that with Susan, because she doesn't ask what I think.

"The reason they're a good idea is that you're forced to come to terms with exactly how much you're eating," she says. "And the only way to change your eating habits is to start by finding out what you eat, how much, and when. Who hasn't sat in front of the TV munching on potato chips, only to find out that by the end of the show the bag is empty and you didn't realize you had eaten that much."

Generalized shoulder-shrugging.

"Exactly," she says. "It's the unconscious eating that we're trying to get away from."

The point isn't that we need to keep food diaries at camp where all the portions are controlled, the idea is that when we go home, we have the tools to help us keep off the weight.

"But everybody cheats on those things," Bunny says.

Faith and I exchange glances.

"That's why we pair you up with buddies when you get home," she says. "And you're going to talk about things like that. Obviously we can't police you 24/7, but we hope that you'll police yourselves because you'll be motivated to keep off the weight that you lost while you were here." There are follow-up phone calls from camp, a newsletter, questionnaires, even the chance for telephone calls with a nutritionist.

Carla sits next to me. The camp is certainly policing her. She's on new pills now that seem to be helping more than the useless old ones. Either that or she's trying to act with-it because she can't face leaving and being home alone. Then again, maybe Trevor has something to do with her improved color. She sneaked out to meet him a few times at night, and he's been sending her notes via a handyman who shuttles back and forth between our camp and the boys'.

Susan passes out lined books with examples of journals that were kept by some of her students during the school year. I knew they'd end up on my diet bookshelf along with *The 3-Hour Diet, The 6-Day Body Makeover, The Fast Track One-Day Detox Diet,* and *The Last Diet Book*—which isn't.

TWENTY-TWO

It's not as though we don't know who the boys are by now or what they look like. But that's the rational take, and at seven o'clock at night, an hour before our next social, the bunk is—HELLO—anything but rational.

Three of us look like we're waiting to audition for Blue Man Group. Bunny offered us her blue pore-minimizing gel that's supposed to dry down after twenty minutes. I suppose it's out of date or something and maybe that's why it got shipped to T.J. Maxx, because after forty it's not only still sticky, it has the consistency of puke. Meanwhile, Summer and Faith have high-lighted their hair and done their toes, so they're strut-ting around like alien creatures with tinfoil wedges sticking out of their heads and toilet paper woven between their toes.

Then there's the clothes issue. The detailed CLOTHES TO BRING list that the camp sent us months *before* camp failed to *suggest* bringing clothing in different sizes, so now most of us are, what, at least one size smaller? Bottom line: Everything we brought looks humongously baggy and butt-ugly.

"This truly sucks," Carla yells, yanking a T-shirt off her head and literally tearing it in half. I don't think she's lost or gained, but she must see something that we don't. Faith shimmies out of a skirt that hangs around her ass "like a sack" and kicks it under the bed.

Add to the equation the fact that three of us could have sold our bodies to PMS researchers. Weird as it is, there's some sort of bizarre scientific thing where girls who live together start to menstruate in sync. I can't for the life of me understand that, but whatever, I swear to you that it's true.

So, short of sharing cyanide-laced lemonade, we're left to make the best of the rags we have using Scotch tape, hidden safety pins, and gynormous hem stitches to alter the fit.

What I end up wearing: Faith's red halter top and my

old, trusty jeans, which have gotten smaller, thanks to the camp laundry witch, who this time came through for me.

What Faith wears: jeans and my black Express top, which looks better on her because she fills it out in the right places and I don't.

What Summer wears: a sequined silver tank top that she had obviously hidden from all of us, because someone, no doubt, would have borrowed it by now.

What Carla wears: a short lilac slip dress with matching sandals. What Bunny wears: The textbook-case how-to-dress-thin look—black jeans, black fitted T-shirt, black high-heeled sandals.

Karen pops her head in and glances around the bunk and then at the floor, which is carpeted with piles of reject clothes.

"Looking good," she says, then adds, "NOT," while shaking her head in disbelief.

Jesse is there already and I wave. I motion that I'm going inside. "Water," I mouth. I stand in line, waiting my turn, watching Carla almost lip-lock with Trevor the instant she sees him. They make a perfect couple. When she's with him, I see a side of her that I don't see in the bunk. She seems relaxed, even flirty. I guess love is a tranquilizer.

I look over at Faith, who as usual, is dancing solo. Bunny is taking turns with Rick as DJ. She's got a monstrous crush on him, but she hasn't gotten to first base yet—or at least that's what she told Summer, who told everybody. And speaking of Summer, she is nowhere to be seen.

I pick up water and a cup of watermelon, and go out to join Jesse. He's against the fence, the same place he positioned himself last time, sitting on the floor once again with his guitar. Only now two things are different.

1. He's wearing a very cool Aerosmith T-shirt instead of the White Stripes one.
2. He isn't alone, and this is definitely *not* cool. Leaning over him, cleavage on display, inches from his face, is Summer.

Only this isn't the bitch queen that I know. This one is coquettish, squealy, a girl who sprinkles her sentences with "SO AMAZING!" and "AWESOME!" I stand back, taking this all in.

What I want to do: Take the fruit salad and shove it down her cleavage. Everybody knows that Jesse and I are (were?) a couple. So why is she pulling this?

What I do: Casually walk over and kneel down, the

third wheel. Does Jesse mind Summer being in his face? Not from what I can see.

"You're AMAZING," Summer coos, almost hitting heads with him. "I used to sing in a band," she says, like an afterthought. "Did I ever tell you, Cam?" The edges of her lips curl into a smile.

"Uh, nooo, I don't think so."

She brightens. "In Wisconsin, we used to sing at these cool parties after the football games." Her head swivels back to Jesse. "Maybe we could sing together on talent night. What do you think?"

"Maybe," he says, his eyes fixating on her briefly. He glances over at me and then back at her and shrugs. "I don't know." He plays one song then another, while we sit there like groupies, afraid to speak. Finally he takes his guitar off over his head and gets to his feet.

"I'll be back." I look up at him to get some signal that he knows what's going on, but all I get is a blank look and a mumbled, "Going to the john."

We sit there tight-lipped. Then the slow count in my head:

O-N-E—T-W-O—T-H-R-E-E—F-O-U-R—F-I-V-E—S-I-X—S-E-V-E-N—E-I-G-H-T—N-I-N-E—T-E-N.

The breather has done nothing—nada, zilch—to allow me to rein in my rage at Summer, who's obliviously coiling her hair around her fingers, trying to mess it up·in a kind of tousled, sexy way, only she doesn't know how transparent it is.

"You are beyond pathetic" comes out in a strained whisper.

"Why?" she asks, incredulously. She shakes her head. "Jesse and I have a lot in common," she says, shooting me the arrogant look that by now I know she wears after she's been attacked. Maybe someone of higher moral ground would leave it at that. But at that moment, I want to mud-wrestle, so I spit my words out:

"All the vomiting in the world won't turn you into a human being, so you should just stay fat—at least you'll have an excuse."

She stares back at me, stung, her face shutting down. I get to my feet and run inside, eyes on the bathroom door so that I'll spot him as soon as he comes out. The moment I do, I start to walk across the crowded dance floor. We need to be alone, to talk. Am I crazy to react this way? Does it matter how she acted to him? He likes me; at least I think he did. Except now I can't think straight at all and everything is swirling around in my head and I'm beginning to wonder if I made up the whole thing about Jesse really liking me. Is it all over now and my problem is that

I just can't see what's in front of me? All I know is that I have to get past everybody and reach him and get out of this hot, crowded, sweaty place.

I push past dancing couples and get jostled one way and then another as different people bump into me, oblivious to the fact that I'm not dancing and am just trying to cross the room. Finally, I'm just feet from Jesse, but the music is so loud that he can't hear me calling him. I watch him walk the other way, over toward the tub of ice, and see him take out two bottles of water, and that's when I stop, because I'm getting this weird, uneasy feeling. He knows I already have water, because I told him I was getting some before I sat down. So it's pretty obvious who the second bottle that he's holding is for. Without him seeing me, I walk back outside and run into the darkness.

TWENTY-THREE

Dear Evie:

Forget everything that I said about starting to like being here, and that goes for everything that I said about Jesse, too. I feel like such a complete jerk. This place is a prison, and I truly wish there was an isolation bunk— somewhere you could go hide and have your meals delivered, slipped through an opening in the door so that you'd never have to see anyone.

Do you remember the bulimic with the bitchy personality I told you about? She tried to hit on Jesse in a big way. And what did he do? Let's just say he didn't push her away.

I can't believe that I came here voluntarily. What id-

iots we were not to insist on staying in the city where there are movies, restaurants, stores, and real life, and no one whipping you to do things that you don't want to do. With all the money that our parents spent to send us away, we could have bought thousands of CDs at the Virgin Megastore and just stayed in our AIR-CONDITIONED, BUG-FREE rooms listening to them or just vegging out and watching television. Live and learn.

   Can't wait to see you!
   Love, Cam

Nobody talks much about the social the morning after. The novelty of being "with the boys" has worn thin. If you haven't hooked up with anyone by now, it's pretty obvious that you probably won't, unless you're like Summer and you set your sights on stealing someone else's boyfriend.

Bunny doesn't really seem to mind. She's accepted the Rick thing. Aside from once crashing her boat into his, she doesn't act as though she cares. Neither does Faith. She spends as much time thinking about her animals as she does about meeting someone who has two legs instead of four.

During lunch, though, something happens that

changes Faith's world, and it has nothing to do with what is going on in camp. Karen comes to our table and tells Faith that she has a phone call. That has never happened before. It's camp policy just to take a message, tell you, and then arrange for you to return the call during the allowed phone hours. So Faith looks up at Karen, surprised, and then gets up and runs to the office. At the end of the meal we hang around for a few extra minutes, waiting to see what the call was all about. But Faith never comes back to the table to explain. In fact, we don't see her again at all until it's free period.

When I get back in the bunk, I see that she's already there. But she's not sitting in her bed writing letters or changing her toenail polish. She's in her bed, curled up in a fetal position. She doesn't turn around when the rest of us walk in; she stays like that, without moving.

"Faith, what's wrong?" I climb the ladder and lean over her. Even though she's the same age as all of us, Faith seems older because she's the strong one in the bunk, the survivor we always turn to. It has to be something terrible.

She shakes her head back and her eyes pool with tears that run back along her cheeks, leaving tiny wet spots on her pillow. She turns to me.

"Brandy was hit by a truck," she whispers as though

using a louder voice would make it more so. "He was playing with another dog and they started to chase each other. He knows to stay away from traffic, but this time he was playing so hard I guess he didn't realize he was out too far. A pickup was speeding along. He hit him and never even stopped."

I look up at the pictures of Brandy that Faith has taped all over the wall near her bed. There are five of him inside her house, outside, with Faith in her bed. He has mottled brown, black, and white fur and keen blue eyes. He's an Australian shepherd, a breed known for being smart, she told me.

Faith's animals are her life. She has an album filled with pictures of them, the way other girls collect pictures of rock stars. I even heard her on the phone one night insisting that her brother "put Brandy on." Then she laughed and talked to him, telling him how much she missed him. She said he barked into the phone and that he knew it was her. She talked back to him and there was silence on the line, as though he were listening.

"Is he . . . dead?"

She shakes her head. "He's in surgery, at the vet's. They don't know if he's going to make it."

I stroke her hair, smoothing it down, away from her face. I don't want her to see the tears that are forming in my eyes. "We're going to pray for him," I say, "all of us." I pause to catch my breath. "I read an article about distant prayer and how people who were in a hospital who had people pray for them—even if they didn't know the people—did better than the ones who didn't have people praying for them. So tonight, instead of talking about ourselves, we're going to send that group energy to Brandy."

Faith nods and then rolls over, hiding her face in the pillow. She doesn't get up for dinner.

TWENTY-FOUR

Anger and frustration seem to give me superior powers of endurance. Water aerobics, hiking, gymnastics, swimming, rowing—let me at them. I need to vent my rage at so many targets: pickup truck drivers who hit dogs and drive off; truck drivers who drink and get behind the wheel; and then Summer and Jesse, with the memories of the social playing like a tape that got stuck and keeps repeating itself in my head. I thought that I had a pretty good eye for understanding relationships—but the exception is when I'm in them.

I can do thirty minutes of running on the treadmill now without getting winded. If it was air-conditioned, I could go a lot longer. And when I hike, I don't get winded either. Fred was right, and it makes me feel more powerful to know that, at least physically, I'm getting into much better shape. I think about my parents and how hard they work out each day and, yes, it does make you feel more positive about yourself.

"Use it or lose it," as my bio teacher used to say.

There is no way to avoid Summer, but I do whatever is humanly possible to keep space between us. If she sits on one side of the mess hall table, I sit on the other. Whenever possible, I'm last in line to make sure I know where she is so that I can avoid her. I'm not sure when the next social is, but I've decided that I'm definitely going to sit it out to avoid seeing her play her game as much as to avoid Jesse.

When there's someone I hate, I always do something completely sick. I ask myself if I saw a bus approaching them, about to hit them, and I had the power to push them out of the way and save them, would I? I guess it's like my mind meter that gauges the extent of my hatred. And with Summer? I wasn't sure.

She was losing weight faster than anyone. At the weigh-in, Faith tells me that she's dropped more than forty-five pounds. I also heard that the nurse asked to talk with her. It was too much weight, too soon. They knew there was something sick and pathetic about her.

"Good," I tell Faith, who's the only one I told about the social. "Maybe they'll send her packing."

"It's hard to hate her," Faith says, who has only good bones in her body. "She's a pretty sad case."

Aside from the weight loss, right before our eyes Summer is actually morphing into the "after" girl she promised to become at the beginning of camp. It's as though she has a checklist and she's ticking off the items, one by one:

1. Hair—It's shorter now, because she went into town one day with Karen and had it trimmed and layered— au revoir to the scraggly ends.
2. Hair color—from mousy brown to blond, thanks to Clairol.
3. Eye lids—now shadowed in smoky brown.
4. Eyes—now rimmed with brown pencil.
5. Cheeks—now pink and vibrant, not pale and lifeless

The only give-away? Her nails. They're still bitten down to the quick, because she can't stop the nervous gnawing and nibbling.

I skip one period at the newspaper office (we kept our jobs, after all), explaining to Karen that I don't feel well.

"Jesse can handle it," I tell her. She promises to give him the message. I never hear anything back, and the paper comes out, so it's obvious that he did all the writing. But now a week has gone by and I can't think up another excuse. While I consider quitting, the easiest way out, I realize that they probably won't find anyone to take my place. Of course they could stick him with the entire job—it would serve him right.

At the end of rowing, I make my way to the office. I'm half hoping that this time *he* won't show. It's empty when I get there, and I go through the list of story suggestions that Lillian left for us. Ever since our quizzes, they decided to *help out* by suggesting stories to make sure that we stayed in the realm of what they thought was acceptable. So much for freedom of the press. I look at the list and shake my head. Could these people be less imaginative? Their suggestions are lethally dull or in the words of our school newspaper editor, MEGOs, which stands for "my eyes glaze over":

1. Low-cal entertaining
2. How I motivate myself to eat a healthy diet
3. Strategies for eating well during the holidays

And then the topper:

4. Feeding extra food to your pet

I turn the sheet into a paper airplane and send it sailing across the room. Then I turn on my computer. But instead of working, I go to a game site and start playing solitaire. When the screen door slams, I jerk back from the desk.

"Hey, Cam," Jesse says.

I ignore him and keep playing.

He leans over and kisses the top of my head. "Thanks for ditching me."

That gets my attention. I swivel around and turn to look up at him. "Excuse me?"

"Thanks for ditching me."

"When was that?"

"At the social," he says.

"That's not the way I remember it."

"You lost me."

"You were enjoying Summer's cleavage just before you got up to go to the bathroom."

"Now I get it."

"I bet you did. So how was she?"

He exhales. "Oh, Jesus."

"I went inside to look for you, but you were busy

getting water for yourself and for her, so I left. What was I supposed to do?"

He stands there, leaning against the side of his desk with his hands tucked deep down into his pockets. He's wearing a bright yellow T-shirt that's fitted, and dammit, I can't stand that I'm attracted to him and the fact that I'm feeling as though a drug is starting to course through my body and take hold of my blood and there's no stopping it. There's no doubt that the exercise has made a difference. He takes his hands from his pockets and begins to rub his eyes, and then he stops and looks at me.

"I got up because she was making me squirm," he says, shaking his head. "I thought you'd follow me and we'd split."

I look back at him to see if he's telling me the truth. He stares at me levelly.

"Really?"

He nods. "Really."

Neither one of us says anything.

"But she was good for something," he says, finally.

I looked at him uncertainly. "Oh, what was that?"

"Making you jealous."

"You see that plane?" I ask, pointing to where it crashed down on the floor. He nods. "It's Lillian's list. That's your punishment—they want an article on strategies for eating well during the holidays."

"How the hell would I know?" he says, protesting. "I usually end up alone, at McDonald's. My dad's always on the road."

"Make it up—nobody will read it anyway."

TWENTY-FIVE

F aith and I ask Mel if we can miss aerobics. We want to use a computer to research the effects of distant prayer. He looks at us for a minute and doesn't say anything. Then his eyes soften and he nods.

I don't understand half of what I read about studies that are blind and double-blind, but I guess the idea is that if an experiment's going to work, some of the people doing it aren't told which people are in which group, because that could affect how they treat them and how things turn out.

It isn't like we have the time to read a million articles, and it isn't as though we're doctors so we'd understand them all if we did. To make it worse, none of the results of the studies are totally black and white. And then there's the fact that some of the groups were small, maybe too small to answer the questions that the studies asked. Still, even when the studies had just a few patients, the ones who were prayed for—even by people far away and by people that they didn't know—seem to come out better.

One study concludes with the words *"the results are encouraging,"* and that's what we walk away with. Should it have mattered to us that the studies were done with people, not dogs? It didn't. At ten o'clock at night, all of us sit on the floor and turn our flashlights up to the ceiling. I'm sitting next to Faith, and Carla's sitting on the other side of her. We all hold hands to form a circle.

"We're going to pray for Brandy," I say, as if I'm the medium. "We're going to close our eyes and imagine him in the hospital, and we're going to send all our group energy to him so that he pulls through and gets well."

Faith squeezes my hand so tightly that I think my fingers will break. We sit there for a few minutes like that. I don't think anyone wants to be the first one to break the circle. Finally, I let go and turn to her.

"He's going to be better, you'll see."

"Cam's right," Summer says. I turn to her. She's looking directly at me. For once, she sounds genuine.

"I'm thinking of him wearing that white coat," Carla

says. "It's a small one. A dog size," she says, making Faith laugh for the first time. "And he's got his paws through it so the little guy's not scared anymore."

Bunny starts to cry, and Summer does too.

"And you've got to wear the white coat too," I tell Faith, squeezing her hand. She looks up at the yellow beams of light, and squeezes her eyes shut.

TWENTY-SIX

I think that Jesse is staring at the computer screen trying to come up with an article for the paper. Then I see that he's staring at a letter. He slips it in front of me.

It's handwritten, and I look at the bottom and see that it's from his dad. He says that he wants to pick Jesse up from camp at the end of the summer.

"He wants another chance," I say.

Jesse doesn't say anything.

"Did you answer him?"

He shakes his head.

"What are you going to say?"

He smirks. "That he's sixteen years too late?"

"He made a move; he's trying. You probably have more in common than you think."

"Yeah, like what?"

I look at him for a minute before answering. "Your mother left him too. It had to hurt him as badly as it hurt you."

He stares at me for a long time and doesn't say anything. "There's something that I didn't tell you."

I wait.

"The person she ran off with . . ."

"What?"

"It was . . . one of the players on my father's team."

I look at him, not sure what to say.

"The guy was about twelve years younger than she is, just a few years out of college. It was all over the TV and in the newspapers." He looks at me, and his eyes are hard. "Do you know how hard that was for a ten-year-old kid to find out and go through . . . alone, because my dad was never around?"

"Yeah," I whisper, trying not to show him all the emotions I am feeling. "At least he finally recognizes that something's wrong."

"But how can he fix it now?"

"Maybe he can't, but how can you not give him a chance?"

TWENTY-SEVEN

Dear Evie:

Home in a week—I can't believe we'll be able to see each other again and hang out and have sleepovers. You asked how I look? I hate it when people brag, but seriously, I have to admit I do look a lot better. Thirty-five pounds lighter, and in good enough shape to run a couple of miles (hilly ones) and not slump over and die. But the big news isn't about me. Listen to this: Jesse's dad wants to be "a real father," he says. He's leaving his New York team, and he told the newspapers that he's not sure what his next job will be. He's had lots of other offers, Jesse told me, but so far, he's turned them all down.

Maybe that's because his next major job will be patching up his relationship with his son.

   Can't wait for you to meet Jesse. I know you'll think he's so cool. Never thought that things would turn out this way. Counting the days until I see you.
Love, Cam

A few days after Faith got the phone call, she got good news and bad news about Brandy. The good news was that he made it through the surgery. The vet told her parents that it helped that he was young and strong and a fighter. He said he was hopeful. Brandy was already home, recuperating.

But the bad news was that Brandy had lost a leg.

Faith looked like she'd been beaten up when she heard. "I don't want to, but I pity him," she told me after she got off the phone with her mother. "He doesn't seem to understand why he can't walk the way he used to."

"Well, at least he isn't as sophisticated as we are," I say. "We know that he won't torture himself. . . . He'll deal."

Talking about Faith's dog made me think about my parents' promise. The day that I got back—I had their word—we were going to drive out to the animal shelter on Long Island and pick out a dog. They agreed to it on the phone, and I sent them a letter asking both of them to sign a pledge, promising. I went to the post office and paid to have it sent with a signed return receipt. I put that into safekeeping in my jewelry box.

Just six days left before our last day of camp, and we go down to the mess hall for breakfast. After we finish our cold cereal with fresh fruit, Summer looks at all of us.

"I'm leaving today," she says, her voice quivering.

"What are you talking about?" Bunny says.

"I'm going into the hospital," she says. "I have . . . problems . . . from the weight loss."

"I'm so sorry," Faith says, as usual, taking the lead. We all murmur in agreement.

"Give me your address," Bunny says. "I'll write to you."

"I'll give you my home address," Summer says. "But I don't know when I'll be there."

"What do you mean?" Carla asks.

"I'm going to a treatment center, like a hospital," Summer says.

Almost solemnly, we walk her back to the bunk without speaking. We sit on the edges of our beds watching her as she packs her clothes. She looks smaller to me now, and for the first time, more vulnerable. I look at her leaning down, pick up her clothes from the floor, and I see the dark roots of her bleached-blond hair.

I don't know much about bulimia, except for hearing

about how constant binging and purging can cause swelling in your throat and eventually heart and bone problems that can't be reversed. Is that what happened to her? I have no way of knowing, and I'm afraid to ask. I keep thinking about our first day at camp and how Summer vowed that when she got home, no one would recognize her. "Before" and "after," she said, making quotation marks with her fingers. The sad part was that now she probably was as different inside as out.

I get up and go over to her, standing at the end of her bed until she looks up at me, surprised. I'm sure that I'm the last one she expected a reaction from. We haven't made as much as eye contact since the night of the social, two weeks before.

"I'm sorry for what you're going through." She's folding a pair of jeans and she stops and looks up at me. She seems uncertain. Maybe she isn't sure if I'm serious. I think back to what I said to her and feel uncomfortable. I shake my head up and down. "I mean it. I hope things work out for you."

She looks at me and her eyes soften. "Thanks, Cam," she says. "And . . . I'm sorry for what I did. It was mean . . . and terrible. I'm ashamed, really," she says, her eyes getting moist. "You were right to hate me."

I shrug. "Maybe we can write letters. I'll give you my address."

She nods, and picks up the jeans that she's been fold-ing. She holds them to her and smoothes them over, again and again. Summer's aunt comes into the bunk and helps her carry out her bags. She waves to all of us, then turns and walks quickly out the door.

"What a bummer," Bunny says, in almost a whisper.

"We never knew who she really was," Carla says. There's a silence in the bunk, and then I see Faith shak-ing her head. "I don't think she knew either," she says.

TWENTY-EIGHT

I don't exactly know what I'm feeling as I fold my last pair of shorts and stuff them inside my trunk. I sit on the edge of my bed and glance around the bunk, which now has been stripped of all the rock posters and snapshots and souvenirs of our lives (even Bunny's recipe for pasta *alla* vodka, which, HEL-LO, does *not*, uh, belong here).

There are no more sandals or sneakers strewn around the bunk, no orphaned socks, no abandoned tubes of hair mousse or gel, or contraband candy bars. Everything is irritatingly tidy, unlike real life.

I really despise good-byes. All kinds. There's all this baggage about the unknown. Will we ever meet again?

Will we be different people when we do? Will good things happen? Bad?

It's deafeningly quiet in the bunk. Faith is taking down the last picture of Brandy and neatly folding back the sides of the tape. Bunny is filling her backpack with magazines for the bus ride home, and Carla is trying to fix a zipper on her Juicy hoodie that has jammed. If I had to guess, I'd say she was about fifteen seconds away from ripping the whole thing into shreds.

"So I'd just like to say that we will *not* be going into long, nauseating, drama-queen style good-byes," I announce to no one in particular, because I can't stand that I haven't heard a peep from anyone about the fact that in less than fifteen minutes we will all be out of the door, on the road, going to homes in different places, and we may never see one another again.

"There will be no long portal good-byes," Faith says.

"What does that mean?" Bunny asks.

"It means . . . um . . . I guess it means that we won't stand in the doorway saying good-bye like forever," Faith says. "I got that expression from my dad," she says, shrugging.

"What we will do," I say.

"1. Write
 2. E-mail

3. IM
4. Call."

"Definitely," Carla says. Somehow, magically, she has fixed the zipper and is now putting on the hoodie. She walks to the middle of the bunk and motions for all of us to join her. We form a kind of huddle, like football players do before the game when I suppose they're praying for victory, or at least not to get their heads busted. Otherwise they're plotting strategy about kicking butt.

"Please, let's not say anything deep and meaningful," I say, denying the wave of emotion that's building up in my throat.

"Amen," Bunny says.

"Why not?" Carla asks. It's obvious that she doesn't get it. Or if she does, she's a lot stronger than I gave her credit for.

"You girls really rock," Faith comes up with, finally.

Then, at that moment, with no further provocation, I do the unthinkable. I start to sob like a pathetic baby and can't stop. A moment later, Bunny, Faith, and Carla join me, and we're crying and crying together like we're at a funeral instead of just the last day of sleep-away camp, and it doesn't stop until a disembodied voice from somewhere outside the bunk calls out in a discordantly cheery manner: "Everybody ready to hit the road?"

We greet the voice with silence. Finally Bunny wipes her eyes and looks around at all of us. "Good-bye, sisters," she says, going for the theatrical. Faith just holds up her hands and we exchange high-fives. I stuff a soggy, balled-up tissue into my pocket, grab my backpack, and run for the bus. I counted on losing weight—I didn't count on losing three of my best friends.

At least on the return trip, Carla is there to keep me company. I realize right then that she's wearing the same pink Juicy outfit that she wore the day we came to camp. I also notice that at some point during the summer, she lost her fixation with repeatedly putting on lip gloss.

Once again, iPods come out. So do copies of *Teen Vogue, Seventeen, Cosmo,* and chick-lit novels. Nothing has changed and everything has. Out of the blue, a strange question comes to mind: How much less does the entire bus weigh now?

TWENTY-NINE

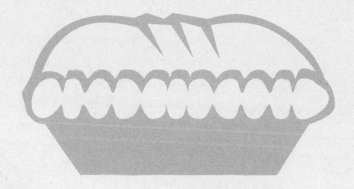

The animal shelter is on Long Island, about a forty-five-minute drive from Manhattan. We enter a spacious area with cages in a big circle around a central atrium. My parents and I walk from one cage to another, looking at the animals who all need homes and all have different stories about how they got there that read like a sad animal soap opera. One was found crouching near a half-abandoned house. Another was treated cruelly by his former owner and removed. A third was brought in by a guy who joined the Marines and is going to Iraq. We look at them all and then go into an adjacent room where they keep the puppies who are adopted much faster.

We have no idea what kind of dog we want. We've

never had one before, but we decide that we'll get one who has already been housebroken, so that we don't have to take him or her out to the curb in the middle of the night.

"How about this one?" my mom asks, stopping in front of a Golden Retriever who jumps up to lick her hand when she puts her fingers through the bars to rub his head. "Cute," I say, but I move on. My father wanders around looking at different dogs and stops in front of each of their cages to study them. Neither of my parents had dogs when they were growing up, so we are all going on some type of gut instinct rather than serious canine knowledge.

"Are you sure you don't want a cat?" my father asks, trying one more time. He is sold on the idea of a cat because you don't have to walk it and you can go out for the day without worrying about coming home to take it out.

"I'm sure." I leave it at that.

I circle the room and then circle it again, waiting for the right feeling. Finally, I stop in front of a cage that I must have missed before. There's a medium-size dog inside. His fur is mostly dark brown, and it's clear that he's a mixed breed, some Lab, some shepherd, something else. I lean over to read about him and see that he is almost two years old and was found at the side of a road.

The sad and strange thing, although there is no explanation, is that he has only three legs. I stand there looking at him and he's looking back at me. Neither of us is moving—it's as though we're both taking each other's measure.

"This one," I say, finally, calling my parents over, feeling the excitement building inside me. "I found the one I want." My parents come over and kneel in front of the cage and look in. They exchange sympathetic looks.

"It's going to be harder," my mom says gently, "but you know that."

"Right . . . I do."

His name is Buddy, but I decide to change it to another name that also starts with a *b*, Brandy. A volunteer from the shelter lets me take him for a walk, and he seems to follow as though he knows how to walk on a leash. He doesn't have the easiest time walking, but he does it, and he seems happy. He goes back into his cage while we fill out the papers and the shelter checks the references that we give them. Finally, the same volunteer goes back to the cage.

"Brandy," he says, patting his head. "You're going home now."

After the adoption, the first thing that I do is invite Evie to sleep over. In keeping with tradition, I grab the take-out

Chinese restaurant menu and start circling what I want—although now I circle half of the dishes that I did before. Then I open the pull-out futon in my room and put three pillows on it: one for me, one for her, and one for Brandy.

When Evie rings the doorbell, Brandy starts barking, and I run to answer it. I open it and stand back for a moment, startled. It's Evie, but a different Evie. She's put on weight. A lot.

Every day after school now, I try to go running in the park. Evie usually joins me, although I'm in better shape than she is. Sometimes Jesse comes with us, and sometimes he just comes over to my house after school and hangs out. His dad volunteered to coach the basketball team at Jesse's school, and as you can imagine, the entire sports department now think they've died and gone to heaven. I ask Jesse if he joined the team, and he laughs. "No way," he says, shaking his head. But he tells me that sometimes "I just hang out, play the guitar, and wait for him to finish." Then, he says, "We go home and eat dinner together."

Next summer, I'm thinking about going back to Camp Calliope. Jesse says he'll go if I do. Evie's thinking about it, too. But what it all depends on is Mel, and whether he lets Brandy join my parents on visiting day.

THIRTY

Now that I've been home from camp for awhile and everyone has noticed that I lost weight and commented on how "amazing" I look, the dust starts to settle and real life starts up again. I'm back at the movies, watching people eating gallon-size cartons of popcorn and jumbo boxes of candy. I find myself left ordering pizza when my parents call me to say they're working late and won't be home for dinner. And I'm back to walking Manhattan streets where every corner has a sign that reads THE ORIGINAL RAY'S PIZZA, displaying calzones and eppie rolls, and every block has a coffee shop window filled with Texas-size muffins. I'm invited to birthday parties where no one else seems worried about calories, and hey, before I turn around it'll be Thanksgiving, or Christmas, or New Year's, and what's a holiday without a huge dinner?

So the question I think about is how many kids go to weight-loss camps and keep off the weight? I hit Google and find out that the answer really isn't clear. One camp said that a year later about 75 percent of kids who answered a progress report said that they had kept the weight off. Another claimed it was 82 percent. But what about the kids who didn't respond because they didn't keep it off and didn't want to admit it? Did they gain back what they lost? Did they gain more? Somewhere I read that the average kid loses about thirty-five pounds in weight-loss camp. Another figure said that during the school year, the average gain is forty pounds.

And our bunk? Faith called last week and told me that she was already feeling frustrated. Her family loves barbecue, she said, and her mom has a way of loading up her plate. She gained one, well, almost two pounds after four weeks home, she added, almost as an afterthought, just before we hung up.

And Bunny—surprise, surprise—signed up for a cordon bleu cooking class after school, according to her last e-mail. She said that she wants to be a pastry chef. I don't recall ever seeing a skinny pastry chef, do you? In our online discussion of how well we were maintaining our weight, I noticed that she didn't comment.

As you can imagine, Carla hasn't gained an ounce since she's been home, thanks to the fact that she's on the track team and runs miles every day after school. She must be on the right mix of medications now, because she told me that she's finally feeling happier about herself.

I wrote to Summer, but she didn't answer. I thought that maybe she was still mad at me, but Faith said that her letter didn't get answered either. No one has heard from her, not even the nutritionist at the camp, who tries to keep in touch with everyone. All my anger at her has vanished, and right now, the only emotion that I feel for her is pity.

As for me, I know the cards are stacked against me and that I'm a prisoner to my genes, because they have a lot to do with how much I want to eat and when. So I'm strong some days and weak on others. When I get mad, the first thing I do is think about going home and eating. Old habits die hard. But now I try to distract myself or make myself wait half an hour before I take a bite of anything.

When I first got home from camp, I kept a scale in my room and used it every day, but now it's inside a bathroom cabinet so that I'm not obsessed with what it says or convinced that if it shows I weigh one pound more that it's a crashing personal failing.

Am I eating less? Overall, yes. Do I try to eat healthier foods? Yes. Have I given up cookies, donuts, cake, ice cream? No. I just try to eat less, and we keep a lot less in the refrigerator now than we did before, so when the weather gets cold and I feel like having a cupcake at ten o'clock at night, I decide that it's not worth the effort to get dressed and walk two blocks to the store in the freezing cold. I am determined to stay in shape. I try to run at least two or three times a week. Jesse also likes to run, and it helps having company.

To keep themselves motivated, some kids tape pictures of high-calorie foods like cake and ice cream up on their refrigerators next to pictures of models in bathing suits, so that every time they reach for the door, they get the message. But I don't put pictures like that on my refrigerator. What I have there is a BEFORE picture of me wearing a baggy black sweatshirt and jeans that are two sizes bigger than the ones I have on now. In the picture, my hair is muddy brown, long, and straight, not layered like it is now, or highlighted, and I'm not wearing any makeup. But what I think of most when I look at that picture is not how fat I look, or how plain. It's the expression on my face. I look sad. Resigned. Even hopeless. I didn't think that my face showed that. I guess that's why they say a camera has an eye.

I lost thirty-five pounds. Thanks to my bunk mates, I learned how to change my hair and wear makeup. And most of all, I spent two months at camp with people who taught me that there are lots of reasons why people gain weight, lots of reasons why they lose it, and lots of reasons why they can or can't keep it off.

So knowing that makes me feel better about myself. Smarter. And stronger. And at least for now, the face that I see in the mirror is a happier one than the picture on the refrigerator.

ABOUT THE AUTHOR

Deborah Blumenthal, an award-winning journalist and nutritionist, divides her time between writing children's books and novels for adults. She has been a regular contributor to the *New York Times*, and her stories have appeared in many other national publications including the *Los Angeles Times*, the *Washington Post*, *Vogue*, *Cosmopolitan*, *Self*, and *Bazaar*. A lifelong New Yorker, she recently moved to Houston. She can be reached on the Web at www.deborahblumenthal.com.